THE SPACE ADVENTURE NOVELS
OF
ANDRE NORTON

SARGASSO OF SPACE
PLAGUE SHIP
VOODOO PLANET and STAR HUNTER
THE CROSSROADS OF TIME
SECRET OF THE LOST RACE
THE SIOUX SPACEMAN

PLAGUE SHIP

BY

ANDRE NORTON

GREGG PRESS
BOSTON

PLAGUE SHIP

This edition published in 1978 by Gregg Press
A Division of G. K. Hall & Co.
by arrangement with Andre Norton

Jacket art by Jack Gaughan
Title page art and design by Elizabeth R. Cooke

Printed on permanent/durable acid-free paper and bound
in the United States of America

First Printing, February 1978

Library of Congress Cataloging in Publication Data

Norton, Andre.
Plague ship.

3 | c 8

(The Space adventure novels of Andre Norton)
Reprint of the 1956 ed. published by Gnome Press,
New York.
I. Title. II. Series.
PZ3.N8187Pl   1978   [PS3527.0625]   813'.5'2   77-25452
ISBN 0-8398-2416-5

CONTENTS

PLAGUE SHIP

chapter 1

PERFUMED PLANET

Dane Thorson, Cargo-master-apprentice of the Solar Queen, Galactic Free Trader spacer, Terra registry, stood in the middle of the ship's cramped bather while Rip Shannon, assistant Astrogator and his senior in the Service of Trade by some four years, applied gobs of highly scented paste to the skin between Dane's rather prominent shoulder blades. The small cabin was thickly redolent with spicy odors and Rip sniffed appreciatively.

"You're sure going to be about the best smelling Terran who ever set boot on Sargol's soil," his soft slur of speech ended in a rich chuckle.

Dane snorted and tried to estimate progress, over one shoulder.

"The things we have to do for Trade!" his comment carried a hint of present embarrassment. "Get it well in—this stuff's supposed to hold for hours. It'd better. According to Van those Salariki can talk your ears right off your head and say nothing worth hearing. And we have to sit and listen until we get a straight answer out of them. Phew!" He shook his head. In such close quarters the scent, pleasing as it was, was also overpowering. "We would have to pick a world such as this—"

Rip's dark fingers halted their circular motion. "Dane," he warned, "don't you go talking against this venture. We got it soft and we're going to be credit-happy—if it works out—"

But, perversely, Dane held to a gloomier view of the immediate future. "*If*," he repeated. "There's a galaxy of 'ifs' in this Sargol proposition. All very well for you to rest easy on your fins—you don't have to run about smelling like a spice works before you can get the time of day from one of the natives!"

Rip put down the jar of cream. "Different worlds, different customs," he iterated the old tag of the Service. "Be glad this one is so easy to conform to. There are some I can think of— There," he ended his massage with a stinging slap, "you're all evenly greased. Good thing you don't have Van's bulk to cover. It takes him a good hour to get his cream on—even with Frank helping to spread. Your clothes ought to be steamed up and ready, too, by now—"

He opened a tight wall cabinet, originally intended to sterilize clothing which might be contaminated by contact with organisms inimical to Terrans. A cloud of steam fragrant with the same spicy scent poured out.

Dane gingerly tugged loose his Trade uniform, its brown silky fabric damp on his skin as he dressed. Luckily Sargol was warm. When he stepped out on its ruby tinted soil this morning no lingering taint of his off-world origin must remain to disgust the sensitive nostrils of the Salariki. He supposed he would get used to this process. After all this was the first time he had undergone the ritual. But he couldn't lose the secret conviction that it was all very silly. Only what Rip had pointed out was the truth—one adjusted to the customs of aliens or one didn't trade and there were other things he might have had to do on other worlds which would have been far more upsetting to that core of private fastidiousness which few would have suspected existed in his tall, lanky frame.

"Whew—out in the open with you—!" Ali Kamil, apprentice-

Engineer, screwed his too regular features into an expression of extreme distaste and waved Dane by him in the corridor.

For the sake of his shipmates' olfactory nerves, Dane hurried on to the port which gave on the ramp now tying the Queen to Sargol's crust. But there he lingered, waiting for Van Rycke, the Cargo-master of the spacer and his immediate superior. It was early morning and now that he was out of the confinement of the ship the fresh morning winds cut about him, rippling through the blue-green grass forest beyond, to take much of his momentary-irritation with them.

There were no mountains in this section of Sargol—the highest elevations being rounded hills tightly clothed with the same ten-foot grass which covered the plains. From the Queen's observation ports, one could watch the constant ripple of the grass so that the planet appeared to be largely clothed in a shimmering, flowing carpet. To the west were the seas—stretches of shallow water so cut up by strings of islands that they more resembled a series of salty lakes. And it was what was to be found in those seas which had lured the Solar Queen to Sargol.

Though, by rights, the discovery was that of another Trader —Traxt Cam—who had bid for trading rights to Sargol, hoping to make a comfortable fortune—or at least expenses with a slight profit—in the perfume trade, exporting from the scented planet some of its most fragrant products. But once on Sargol he had discovered the Koros stones—gems of a new type—a handful of which offered across the board in one of the inner planet trading marts had nearly caused a riot among bidding gem merchants. And Cam had been well on the way to becoming one of the princes of Trade when he had been drawn into the vicious net of the Limbian pirates and finished off.

Because they, too, had stumbled into the trap which was Limbo, and had had a very definite part in breaking up that devilish installation, the crew of the Solar Queen had claimed as their reward the trading rights of Traxt Cam in default of legal heirs. And so here they were on Sargol with the notes left by Cam as their guide, and as much lore concerning the Salariki as was known crammed into their minds.

Dane sat down on the end of the ramp, his feet on Sargolian soil, thin, red soil with glittering bits of gold flake in it. He did not doubt that he was under observation from hidden eyes, but he tried to show no sign that he guessed it. The adult Salariki maintained at all times an attitude of aloof and complete indifference toward the Traders, but the juvenile population were as curious as their elders were contemptuous. Perhaps there was a method of approach in that. Dane considered the idea.

Van Rycke and Captain Jellico had handled the first negotiations—and the process had taken most of a day—the result totaling exactly nothing. In their contacts with the off world men the feline ancestered Salariki were ceremonious, wary, and completely detached. But Cam had gotten to them somehow— or he would not have returned from his first trip with that pouch of Koros stones. Only, among his records, salvaged on Limbo, he had left absolutely no clue as to how he had beaten down native sales resistance. It was baffling. But patience had to be the middle name of every Trader and Dane had complete faith in Van. Sooner or later the Cargo-master would find a key to unlock the Salariki.

As if the thought of Dane's chief had summoned him, Van Rycke, his scented tunic sealed to his bull's neck in unaccustomed trimness, his cap on his blond head, strode down the ramp, broadcasting waves of fragrance as he moved. He sniffed vigorously as he approached his assistant and then nodded in approval.

"So you're all greased and ready—"

"Is the Captain coming too, sir?"

Van Rycke shook his head. "This is our headache. Patience, my boy, patience—" He led the way through a thin screen of the grass on the other side of the scorched landing field to a well-packed earth road.

Again Dane felt eyes, knew that they were being watched. But no Salarik stepped out of concealment. At least they had nothing to fear in the way of attack. Traders were immune, taboo, and the trading stations were set up under the white diamond shield of peace, a peace guaranteed on blood oath by every clan chieftain in the district. Even in the midst of inter-clan feuding deadly enemies met in amity under that shield and would not turn claw knife against each other within a two mile radius of its protection.

The grass forests rustled betrayingly, but the Terrans displayed no interest in those who spied upon them. An insect with wings of brilliant green gauze detached itself from the stalk of a grass tree and fluttered ahead of the Traders as if it were an official herald. From the red soil crushed by their boots arose a pungent odor which fought with the scent they carried with them. Dane swallowed three or four times and hoped that his superior officer had not noted that sign of discomfort. Though Van Rycke, in spite of his general air of sleepy benevolence and careless goodwill, noticed everything, no matter how trivial, which might have a bearing on the delicate negotiations of Galactic Trade. He had not climbed to his present status of expert Cargo-master by overlooking anything at all. Now he gave an order:

"Take an equalizer—"

Dane reached for his belt pouch, flushing, fiercely determined inside himself, that no matter how smells warred about him that day, he was not going to let it bother him. He swallowed the tiny pellet Medic Tau had prepared for just such trials and tried to occupy his mind with the work to come. If there would be any work—or would another long day be wasted in futile speeches of mutual esteem which gave formal lip service to Trade and its manifest benefits?

"Houuuu—" The cry which was half wail, half arrogant warning, sounded along the road behind them.

Van Rycke's stride did not vary. He did not turn his head, show any sign he had heard that heralding fanfare for a clan chieftain. And he continued to keep to the exact center of the road, Dane the regulation one pace to the rear and left as befitted his lower rank.

"Houuu—" that blast from the throat of a Salarik especially chosen for his lung power was accompanied now by the hollow drum of many feet. The Terrans neither looked around nor withdrew from the center, nor did their pace quicken.

That, too, was in order, Dane knew. To the rank conscious Salariki clansmen you did not yield precedence unless you wanted at once to acknowledge your inferiority—and if you did that by some slip of admission or omission, there was no use in trying to treat face to face with their chieftains again.

"Houuu—!" The blast behind was a scream as the retinue it announced swept around the bend in the road to catch sight of the two Traders oblivious of it. Dane longed to be able to turn his head, just enough to see which one of the local lordlings they blocked.

"Houu—" there was a questioning note in the cry now and the heavy thud-thud of feet was slacking. The clan party had seen them, were hesitant about the wisdom of trying to shove them aside.

Van Rycke marched steadily onward and Dane matched his pace. They might not possess a leather-lunged herald to clear their road, but they gave every indication of having the right to occupy as much of it as they wished. And that unruffled poise had its affect upon those behind. The pound of feet slowed to a walk, a walk which would keep a careful distance behind the two Terrans. It had worked—the Salariki—or these Salariki—were accepting them at their own valuation—a good omen for the day's business. Dane's spirits rose, but he schooled his features into a mask as wooden as his superior's. After all this was a very minor victory and they had ten or twelve hours of polite, and hidden, maneuvering before them.

The Solar Queen had set down as closely as possible to the trading center marked on Traxt Cam's private map and the Terrans now had another five minutes march, in the middle of the road, ahead of the chieftain who must be inwardly boiling at their presence, before they came out in the clearing containing the roofless, circular erection which served the Salariki of the district as a market place and a common meeting ground for truce talks and the mending of private clan alliances. Erect on a pole in the middle, towering well above the nodding fronds of the grass trees, was the pole bearing the trade shield which promised not only peace to those under it, but a three day sanctuary to any feuder or duelist who managed to win to it and lay hands upon its weathered standard.

They were not the first to arrive, which was also a good thing. Gathered in small groups about the walls of the council place were the personal attendants, liege warriors, and younger relatives of at least four or five clan chieftains. But, Dane noted at once, there was not a single curtained litter or riding orgel to be seen. None of the feminine part of the Salariki species had arrived. Nor would they until the final trade treaty was concluded and established by their fathers, husbands, or sons.

With the assurance of one who was master in his own clan, Van Rycke, displaying no interest at all in the shifting mass of lower rank Salariki, marched straight on to the door of the enclosure. Two or three of the younger warriors got to their feet, their brilliant cloaks flicking out like spreading wings. But when Van Rycke did not even lift an eyelid in their direction, they made no move to block his path.

As fighting men, Dane thought, trying to study the specimens before him with a totally impersonal stare, the Salariki were an impressive lot. Their average height was close to six feet, their distant feline ancestry apparent only in small vestiges. A Salarik's nails on both hands and feet were retractile, his skin was gray, his thick hair, close to the texture of plushy fur, extended down his backbone and along the outside of his well muscled arms and legs, and was tawny-yellow, blue-gray or white. To Terran eyes the broad faces, now all turned in their direction, lacked readable expression. The eyes were large and set slightly aslant in the skull, being startlingly orange-red or a brilliant turquoise green-blue. They wore loin cloths of brightly dyed fabrics with wide sashes forming corselets about their slender middles, from which gleamed the gem-set hilts of their claw knives, the possession of which proved their adulthood. Cloaks as flamboyant as their other garments hung in bat wing folds from their shoulders and each and every one moved in an invisible cloud of perfume.

Brilliant as the assemblage of liege men without had been, the gathering of clan leaders and their upper officers within the council place was a riot of color—and odor. The chieftains were installed on the wooden stools, each with a small table before him on which rested a goblet bearing his own clan sign, a folded strip of patterned cloth—his "trade shield"—and a gemmed box containing the scented paste he would use for refreshment during the ordeal of conference.

A breeze fluttered sash ends and tugged at cloaks, otherwise the assembly was motionless and awesomely quiet. Still making no overtures Van Rycke crossed to a stool and table which stood a little apart and seated himself. Dane went into the action required of him. Before his superior he set out a plastic pocket flask, its color as alive in the sunlight as the crudely cut gems which the Salariki sported, a fine silk handkerchief, and, last of all, a bottle of Terran smelling salts provided by Medic Tau as a necessary restorative after some hours combination of Salariki oratory and Salariki perfumes. Having thus done the duty of liege man, Dane was at liberty to seat himself, cross-legged on the ground behind his chief, as the other sons, heirs, and advisors had gathered behind their lords.

The chieftain whose arrival they had in a manner delayed came in after them and Dane saw that it was Fashdor—another piece of luck—since that clan was a small one and the chieftain had little influence. Had they so slowed Halfer or Paft it might be a different matter altogether.

Fashdor was established at his seat, his belongings spread out, and Dane, counting unobtrusively, was certain that the council was now complete. Seven clans Traxt Cam had recorded divided the sea coast territory and there were seven chieftains here—indicative of the importance of this meeting since some of these clans, beyond the radius of the shield peace, must be fighting a vicious blood feud at that very moment. Yes, seven were here. Yet there still remained a single stool, directly across the circle from Van Rycke. An empty stool—who was the late comer?

That question was answered almost as it flashed into Dane's

mind. But no Salariki lordling came through the door. Dane's self-control kept him in his place, even after he caught the meaning of the insignia emblazoned across the newcomer's tunic. Trader—and not only a Trader but a Company man! But why—and how? The Companies only went after big game —this was a planet thrown open to Free Traders, the independents of the star lanes. By law and right no Company man had any place here. Unless—behind a face Dane strove to keep as impassive as Van's his thoughts raced. Traxt Cam as a Free Trader had bid for the right to exploit Sargol when its sole exportable product was deemed to be perfume—a small, unimportant trade as far as the Companies were concerned. And then the Koros stones had been found and the importance of Sargol must have boomed as far as the big boys could see. They probably knew of Traxt Cam's death as soon as the Patrol report on Limbo had been sent to Headquarters. The Companies all maintained their private information and espionage services. And, with Traxt Cam dead without an heir, they had seen their chance and moved in. Only, Dane's teeth set firmly, they didn't have the ghost of a chance now. Legally there was only one Trader on Sargol and that was the Solar Queen, Captain Jellico had his records signed by the Patrol to prove that. And all this Inter-Solar man could do now was to bow out and try poaching elsewhere.

But the I-S man appeared to be in no haste to follow that only possible course. He was seating himself with arrogant dignity on that unoccupied stool, and a younger man in I-S uniform was putting before him the same type of equipment Dane had produced for Van Rycke. The Cargo-master of the Solar Queen showed no surprise, if the Eysies' appearance had been such to him.

One of the younger warriors in Paft's train got to his feet and brought his hands together with a clap which echoed across the silent gathering with the force of an archaic solid projectal shot. A Salarik, wearing the rich dress of the upper ranks, but also the collar forced upon a captive taken in combat, came into the enclosure carrying a jug in both hands. Preceded by

Paft's son he made the rounds of the assembly pouring a purple liquid from his jug into the goblet before each chieftain, a goblet which Paft's heir tasted ceremoniously before it was presented to the visiting clan leader. When they paused before Van Rycke the Salarik nobleman touched the side of the plasta flask in token. It was recognized that off world men must be cautious over the sampling of local products and that when they joined in the Taking of the First Cup of Peace, they did so symbolically.

Paft raised his cup, his gesture copied by everyone around the circle. In the harsh tongue of his race he repeated a formula so archaic that few of the Salariki could now translate the singsong words. They drank and the meeting was formally opened.

But it was an elderly Salarik seated to the right of Halfer, a man who wore no claw knife and whose dusky yellow cloak and sash made a subdued note amid the splendor of his fellows, who spoke first, using the click-clack of the Trade Lingo his nation had learned from Cam.

"Under the white," he pointed to the shield aloft, "we assemble to hear many things. But now come two tongues to speak where once there was but one father of a clan. Tell us, outlanders, which of you must we now hark to in truth?" He looked from Van Rycke to the I-S representative.

The Cargo-master from the Queen did not reply. He stared across the circle at the Company man. Dane waited eagerly. What *was* the I-S going to say to that?

But the fellow did have an answer, ready and waiting. "It is true, fathers of clans, that here are two voices, where by right and custom there should only be one. But this is a matter which can be decided between us. Give us leave to withdraw from your sight and speak privately together. Then he who returns to you will be the true voice and there shall be no more division—"

It was Paft who broke in before Halfer's spokesman could reply.

"It would have been better to have spoken together before you came to us. Go then until the shadow of the shield is not,

then return hither and speak truly. We do not wait upon the
pleasure of outlanders—"

A murmur approved that tart comment. "Until the shadow
of the shield is not." They had until noon. Van Rycke arose
and Dane gathered up his chief's possessions. With the same
superiority to his surroundings he had shown upon entering, the
Cargo-master left the enclosure, the Eysies following. But they
were away from the clearing, out upon the road back to the
Queen before the two from the Company caught up with them.

"Captain Grange will see you right away—" the Eysie Cargo-
master was beginning when Van Rycke met him with a quell-
ing stare.

"If you poachers have anything to say—you say it at the
Queen and to Captain Jellico," he stated flatly and started on.

Above his tight tunic collar the other's face flushed, his teeth
flashed as he caught his lower lip between them as if to forcibly
restrain an answer he longed to make. For a second he hesitated and then he vanished down a side path with his assistant.
Van Rycke had gone a quarter of the distance back to the ship
before he spoke.

"I thought it was too easy," he muttered. "Now we're in for
it—maybe right up the rockets! By the Spiked Tail of Exol, this
is certainly *not* our lucky day!" He quickened pace until they
were close to trotting.

chapter 2

RIVALS

"That's far enough, Eysie!"

Although Traders by law and tradition carried no more potent personal weapons—except in times of great crisis—than hand sleep rods, the resultant shot from the latter was just as unpleasant for temporary periods as a more forceful beam—and the threat of it was enough to halt the three men who had come to the foot of the Queen's ramp and who could see the rod held rather negligently by Ali. Ali's eyes were anything but negligent however, and Free Traders had reputations to be respected by their rivals of the Companies. The very nature of their roving lives taught them savage lessons—which they either learned or died.

Dane, glancing down over the Engineer-apprentice's shoulder, saw that Van Rycke's assumption of confidence had indeed paid off. They had left the trade enclosure of the Salariki barely three-quarters of an hour ago. But below now stood the be-badged Captain of the I-S ship and his Cargo-master.

"I want to speak to your Captain—" snarled the Eysie officer.

Ali registered faint amusement, an expression which tended to rouse the worst in the spectator, as Dane knew of old when that same mocking appraisal had been turned on him as the rawest of the Queen's crew.

"But does *he* wish to speak to you?" countered Kamil. "Just stay where you are, Eysie, until we are sure about that fact."

That was his cue to act as messenger. Dane retreated into the ship and swung up the ladder to the command section. As he passed Captain Jellico's private cabin he heard the muffled squall of the commander's unpleasant pet—Queex, the Hoobat —a nightmare combination of crab, parrot and toad, wearing a blue feather coating and inclined to scream and spit at all comers. Since Queex would not be howling in that fashion if its master was present, Dane kept on to the control cabin where he blundered in upon an executive level conference of Captain, Cargo-master and Astrogator.

"Well?" Jellico's blaster scarred left cheek twitched as he snapped that impatient inquiry at the messenger.

"Eysie Captain below, sir. With his Cargo-master. They want to see you—"

Jellico's mouth was a straight line, his eyes very hard. By instinct Dane's hand went to the grip of the sleep rod slung at his belt. When the Old Man put on his fighting face—look out! Here we go again, he told himself, speculating as to just what type of action lay before them now.

"Oh, they do, do they!" Jellico began and then throttled down the temper he could put under iron control when and if it were necessary. "Very well, tell them to stay where they are. Van, we'll go down—"

For a moment the Cargo-master hesitated, his heavy-lidded eyes looked sleepy, he seemed almost disinterested in the suggestion. And when he nodded it was with the air of someone about to perform some boring duty.

"Right, sir." He wriggled his heavy body from behind the small table, resealed his tunic, and settled his cap with as much precision as if he were about to represent the Queen before the assembled nobility of Sargol.

Dane hurried down the ladders, coming to a halt beside Ali. It was the turn of the man at the foot of the ramp to bark an impatient demand:

"Well?" (Was that the theme word of every Captain's vocabulary?)

"You wait," Dane replied with no inclination to give the Eysie officer any courtesy address. Close to a Terran year aboard the Solar Queen had inoculated him with pride in his own section of Service. A Free Trader was answerable to his own officers and to no one else on earth—or among the stars—no matter how much discipline and official etiquette the Companies used to enhance their power.

He half expected the I-S officers to leave after an answer such as that. For a Company Captain to be forced to wait upon the convenience of a Free Trader must be galling in the extreme. And the fact that this one was doing just that was an indication that the Queen's crew did, perhaps, have the edge of advantage in any coming bargain. In the meantime the Eysie contingent fumed below while Ali lounged whistling against the exit port, playing with his sleep rod and Dane studied the grass forest. His boot nudged a packet just inside the port casing and he glanced inquiringly from it to Ali.

"Cat ransom," the other answered his unspoken question.

So that was it—the fee for Sinbad's return. "What is it today?"

"Sugar—about a tablespoon full," the Engineer-assistant returned, "and two colored steelos. So far they haven't run up the price on us. I think they're sharing out the spoil evenly, a new cub brings him back every night."

As did all Terran ships, the Solar Queen carried a cat as an important member of her regular crew. And the portly Sinbad, before their landing on Sargol, had never presented any problem. He had done his duty of ridding the ship of unusual and usual pests and cargo despoilers with dispatch, neatness and energy. And when in port on alien worlds had never shown any inclination to go a-roving.

But the scents of Sargol had apparently intoxicated him, shearing away his solid dignity and middle-aged dependability. Now Sinbad flashed out of the Queen at the opening of her port in the early morning and was brought back, protesting with both voice and claws, at the end of the day by that member of the juvenile population whose turn it was to collect the standing reward for his forceful delivery. Within three days it had become an accepted business transaction which satisfied everyone but Sinbad.

The scrape of metal boot soles on ladder rungs warned of the arrival of their officers. Ali and Dane withdrew down the corridor, leaving the entrance open for Jellico and Van Rycke. Then they drifted back to witness the meeting with the Eysies.

There were no prolonged greetings between the two parties, no offer of hospitality as might have been expected between Terrans on an alien planet a quarter of the Galaxy away from the earth which had given them a common heritage.

Jellico, with Van Rycke at his shoulder, halted before he stepped from the ramp so that the three Inter-Solar men, Captain, Cargo-master and escort, whether they wished or no, were put in the disadvantageous position of having to look up to a Captain whom they, as members of one of the powerful Companies, affected to despise. The lean, well muscled, trim figure of the Queen's commander gave the impression of hard bitten force held in check by will control, just as his face under its thick layer of space burn was that of an adventurer accustomed to make split second decisions—an estimate underlined by that seam of blaster burn across one flat cheek.

Van Rycke, with a slight change of dress, could have been a Company man in the higher ranks—or so the casual observer would have placed him, until such an observer marked the eyes behind those sleepy drooping lids, or caught a certain note in the calm, unhurried drawl of his voice. To look at the two senior officers of the Free Trading spacer were the antithesis of each other—in action they were each half of a powerful, steamroller whole—as a good many men in the Service—scattered over a half dozen or so planets—had discovered to their cost in the past.

Now Jellico brought the heels of his space boots together with an extravagant click and his hand flourished at the fore of his helmet in a gesture which was better suited to the Patrol hero of a slightly out-of-date Video serial.

"Jellico, Solar Queen, Free Trader," he identified himself brusquely, and added, "This is Van Rycke, our Cargo-master."

Not all the flush had faded from the face of the I-S Captain.

"Grange of the Dart," he did not even sketch a salute. "Inter-Solar. Kallee, Cargo-master—" And he did not name the hovering third member of his party.

Jellico stood waiting and after a long moment of silence Grange was forced to state his business.

"We have until noon—"

Jellico, his fingers hooked in his belt, simply waited. And under his level gaze the Eysie Captain began to find the going hard.

"They have given us until noon," he started once more, "to get together—"

Jellico's voice came, coldly remote. "There is no reason for any 'getting together,' Grange. By rights I can have you up before the Trade Board for poaching. The Solar Queen has sole trading rights here. If you up-ship within a reasonable amount of time, I'll be inclined to let it pass. After all I've no desire to run all the way to the nearest Patrol post to report you—"

"You can't expect to buck Inter-Solar. We'll make you an offer—" That was Kallee's contribution, made probably because his commanding officer couldn't find words explosive enough.

Jellico, whose forté was more direct action, took an excursion into heavy-handed sarcasm. "You Eysies have certainly been given excellent briefing. I would advise a little closer study of the Code—and not the sections in small symbols at the end of the tape, either! We're not bucking anyone. You'll find our registration for Sargol down on tapes at the Center. And I suggest that the sooner you withdraw the better—before we cite you for illegal planeting."

Grange had gained control of his emotions. "We're pretty far from Center here," he remarked. It was a statement of fact, but it carried over-tones which they were able to assess correctly. The Solar Queen was a Free Trader, alone on an alien world. But the I-S ship might be cruising in company, ready to summon aid, men and supplies. Dane drew a deep breath, the Eysies *must* be sure of themselves, not only that, but they must want what Sargol had to offer to the point of being willing to step outside the law to get it.

The I-S Captain took a step forward. "I think we understand each other now," he said, his confidence restored.

Van Rycke answered him, his deep voice cutting across the sighing of the wind in the grass forest.

"Your proposition?"

Perhaps this return to their implied threat bolstered their belief in the infallibility of the Company, their conviction that no independent dared stand up against the might and power of Inter-Solar. Kallee replied:

"We'll take up your contract, at a profit to you, and you up-ship before the Salariki are confused over whom they are to deal with—"

"And the amount of profit?" Van Rycke bored in.

"Oh," Kallee shrugged, "say ten percent of Cam's last shipment—"

Jellico laughed. "Generous, aren't you, Eysie? Ten percent of a cargo which can't be assessed—the gang on Limbo kept no records of what they plundered."

"We don't know what he was carrying when he crashed on Limbo," countered Kallee swiftly. "We'll base our offer on what he carried to Axal."

Now Van Rycke chuckled. "I wonder who figured that one out?" he inquired of the scented winds. "He must save the Company a fair amount of credits one way or another. Interesting offer—"

By the bland satisfaction to be read on the three faces below the I-S men were assured of their victory. The Solar Queen would be paid off with a pittance, under the vague threat of Company retaliation she would up-ship from Sargol, and they would be left in possession of the rich Koros trade—to be commended and rewarded by their superiors. Had they, Dane speculated, ever had any dealings with Free Traders before—at least with the brand of independent adventurers such as manned the Solar Queen?

Van Rycke burrowed in his belt pouch and then held out his hand. On the broad palm lay a flat disc of metal. "Very interesting—" he repeated. "I shall treasure this recording—"

The sight of that disc wiped all satisfaction from the Eysie faces. Grange's purplish flush spread up from his tight tunic collar, Kallee blinked, and the unknown third's hand dropped to his sleep rod. An action which was not overlooked by either Dane or Ali.

"A smooth set down to you," Jellico gave the conventional leave taking of the Service.

"You'd better—" the Eysie Captain began hotly, and then seeing the disc Van Rycke held—that sensitive bit of metal and plastic which was recording this interview for future reference, he shut his mouth tight.

"Yes?" the Queen's Cargo-master prompted politely. But Kallee had taken his Captain's arm and was urging Grange away from the spacer.

"You have until noon to lift," was Jellico's parting shot as the three in Company livery started toward the road.

"I don't think that they will," he added to Van Rycke.

The Cargo-master nodded. "You wouldn't in their place," he pointed out reasonably. "On the other hand they've had a bit of a blast they weren't expecting. It's been a long time since Grange heard anyone say 'no.' "

"A shock which is going to wear off," Jellico's habitual distrust of the future gathered force.

"This," Van Rycke tucked the disc back into his pouch, "sent them off vector a parsec or two. Grange is not one of the strong arm blaster boys. Suppose Tang Ya does a little listening in—and maybe we can rig another surprise if Grange does try to ask advice of someone off world. In the meantime I don't think they are going to meddle with the Salariki. They don't want to have to answer awkward questions if *we* turn up a Patrol ship to ask them. So—" he stretched and beckoned to Dane, "we shall go to work once more."

Again two paces behind Van Rycke Dane tramped to the trade circle of the Salariki clansmen. They might have walked out only five or six minutes of ship time before, and the natives betrayed no particular interest in their return. But, Dane noted, there was only one empty stool, one ceremonial table in evidence. The Salariki had expected only one Terran Trader to join them.

What followed was a dreary round of ceremony, an exchange of platitudes and empty good wishes and greetings. No one mentioned Koros stones—or even perfume bark—that he was willing to offer the off-world traders. None lifted so much as a corner of his trade cloth, under which, if he were ready to deal seriously, his hidden hand would meet that of the buyer, so that by finger pressure alone they could agree or disagree on price. But such boring sessions were part of Trade and Dane, keeping a fraction of attention on the speeches and "drinkings-together," watched those around him with an eye which tried to assess and classify what he saw.

The keynote of the Salariki character was a wary independence. The only form of government they would tolerate was a family-clan organization. Feuds and deadly duels between individuals and clans were the accepted way of life and every male who reached adulthood went armed and ready for combat until he became a "Speaker for the past"—too old to bear arms in the field. Due to the nature of their battling lives, relatively few of the Salariki ever reached that retirement. Short-lived alliances between families sometimes occurred, usually when they were to face a common enemy greater than either. But a quarrel between chieftains, a fancied insult would rip that open in an instant. Only under the Trade Shield could seven clans sit this way without their warriors being at one another's furred throats.

An hour before sunset Paft turned his goblet upside down on his table, a move followed speedily by every chieftain in the circle. The conference was at an end for that day. And as far as Dane could see it had accomplished exactly nothing—except to bring the Eysies into the open. What *had* Traxt Cam discovered which had given him the trading contact with these suspicious aliens? Unless the men from the Queen learned it, they could go on talking until the contract ran out and get no farther than they had today.

From his training Dane knew that ofttimes contact with an alien race did require long and patient handling. But between study and experiencing the situation himself there was a gulf, and he thought somewhat ruefully that he had much to learn before he could meet such a situation with Van Rycke's un-failing patience and aplomb. The Cargo-master seemed in no-wise tired by his wasted day and Dane knew that Van would probably sit up half the night, going over for the hundredth time Traxt Cam's sketchy recordings in another painstaking attempt to discover why and how the other Free Trader had succeeded where the Queen's men were up against a stone wall.

The harvesting of Koros stones was, as Dane and all those who had been briefed from Cam's records knew, a perilous job. Though the rule of the Salariki was undisputed on the land masses of Sargol, it was another matter in the watery world of the shallow seas. There the Gorp were in command of the ter-ritory and one had to be constantly alert for attack from that sly, reptilian intelligence, so alien to the thinking processes of both Salariki and Terran that there was, or seemed to be, no point of possible contact. One went gathering Koros gems after balancing life against gain. And perhaps the Salariki did not see any profit in that operation. Yet Traxt Cam had brought back his bag of gems—somehow he had managed to secure them in trade.

Van Rycke climbed the ramp, hurrying on into the Queen as if he could not get back to his records soon enough. But

Dane paused and looked back at the grass jungle a little wistfully. To his mind these early evening hours were the best time on Sargol. The light was golden, the night winds had not yet arisen. He disliked exchanging the freedom of the open for the confinement of the spacer.

And, as he hesitated there, two of the juvenile population of Sargol came out of the forest. Between them they carried one of their hunting nets, a net which now enclosed a quiet but baneful eyed captive—Sinbad being delivered for nightly ransom. Dane was reaching for the pay to give the captors when, to his real astonishment, one of them advanced and pointed with an extended forefinger claw to the open port.

"Go in," he formed the Trade Lingo words with care. And Dane's surprise must have been plain to read for the cub followed his speech with a vigorous nod and set one foot on the ramp to underline his desire.

For one of the Salariki, who had continually manifested their belief that Terrans and their ship were an offence to the nostrils of all right living "men," to wish to enter the spacer was an astonishing about-face. But any advantage no matter how small, which might bring about a closer understanding, must be seized at once.

Dane accepted the growling Sinbad and beckoned, knowing better than to touch the boy. "Come—"

Only one of the junior clansmen obeyed that invitation. The other watched, big-eyed, and then scuttled back to the forest when his fellow called out some suggestion. *He* was not going to be trapped.

Dane led the way up the ramp, paying no visible attention to the young Salarik, nor did he urge the other on when he lingered for a long moment or two at the port. In his mind the Cargo-master apprentice was feverishly running over the list of general trade goods. What *did* they carry which would make a suitable and intriguing gift for a small alien with such a promising bump of curiosity? If he had only time to get Van Rycke!

The Salarik was inside the corridor now, his nostrils spread, assaying each and every odor in this strange place. Suddenly his head jerked as if tugged by one of his own net ropes. His interest had been riveted by some scent his sensitive senses had detected. His eyes met Dane's in appeal. Swiftly the Terran nodded and then followed with a lengthened stride as the Salarik sped down into the lower reaches of the Queen, obviously in quest of something of great importance.

chapter 3

CONTACT AT LAST

"What in—" Frank Mura, steward, storekeeper, and cook of the Queen, retreated into the nearest cabin doorway as the young Salarik flashed down the ladder into his section.

Dane, with the now resigned Sinbad in the crook of his arm, had tailed his guest and arrived just in time to see the native come to an abrupt halt before one of the most important doors in the spacer—the portal of the hydro garden which renewed the ship's oxygen and supplied them with fresh fruit and vegetables to vary their diet of concentrates.

The Salarik laid one hand on the smooth surface of the sealed compartment and looked back over his shoulder at Dane with an inquiry to which was added something of a plea. Guided by his instinct—that this was important to them all—Dane spoke to Mura:

"Can you let him in there, Frank?"

It was not sensible, it might even be dangerous. But every member of the crew knew the necessity for making some sort of contact with the natives. Mura did not even nod, but squeezed by the Salarik and pressed the lock. There was a sigh of air, and the crisp smell of growing things, lacking the languorous perfumes of the world outside, puffed into the faces.

The cub remained where he was, his head up, his wide nostrils visibly drinking in that smell. Then he moved with the silent, uncanny speed which was the heritage of his race, darting down the narrow aisle toward a mass of greenery at the far end.

Sinbad kicked and growled. This was his private hunting ground—the preserve he kept free of invaders. Dane put the cat down. The Salarik had found what he was seeking. He stood on tiptoe to sniff at a plant, his yellow eyes half closed, his whole stance spelling ecstasy. Dane looked to the steward for enlightenment.

"What's he so interested in, Frank?"

"Catnip."

"Catnip?" Dane repeated. The word meant nothing to him, but Mura had a habit of picking up strange plants and cultivating them for study. "What is it?"

"One of the Terran mints—an herb," Mura gave a short explanation as he moved down the aisle toward the alien. He broke off a leaf and crushed it between his fingers.

Dane, his sense of smell largely deadened by the pungency with which he had been surrounded by most of that day, could distinguish no new odor. But the young Salarik swung around to face the steward his eyes wide, his nose questing. And Sinbad gave a whining yowl and made a spring to push his head against the steward's now aromatic hand.

So—now they had it—an opening wedge. Dane came up to the three.

"All right to take a leaf or two?" he asked Mura.

"Why not? I grow it for Sinbad. To a cat it is like heemel smoke or a tankard of lackibod."

And by Sinbad's actions Dane guessed that the plant did hold for the cat the same attraction those stimulants produced in human beings. He carefully broke off a small stem supporting three leaves and presented it to the Salarik, who stared at him and then, snatching the twig, raced from the hydro garden as if pursued by feuding clansmen.

Dane heard the pad of his feet on the ladder—apparently the cub was making sure of escape with his precious find. But the Cargo-master apprentice was frowning. As far as he could see there were only five of the plants.

"That all the catnip you have?"

Mura tucked Sinbad under his arm and shooed Dane before him out of the hydro. "There was no need to grow more. A small portion of the herb goes a long way with this one," he put the cat down in the corridor. "The leaves may be preserved by drying. I believe that there is a small box of them in the galley."

A strictly limited supply. Suppose this was the key which would unlock the Koros trade? And yet it was to be summed up in five plants and a few dried leaves! However, Van Rycke must know of this as soon as possible.

But to Dane's growing discomfiture the Cargo-master showed no elation as his junior poured out the particulars of his discovery. Instead there were definite signs of displeasure to be read by those who knew Van Rycke well. He heard Dane out and then got to his feet. Tolling the younger man with him by a crooked finger, he went out of his combined office-living quarters to the domain of Medic Craig Tau.

"Problem for you, Craig." Van Rycke seated his bulk on the wall jump seat Tau pulled down for him. Dane was left standing just within the door, very sure now that instead of being commended for his discovery of a few minutes before, he was about to suffer some reprimand. And the reason for it still eluded him.

"What do you know about that plant Mura grows in the hydro—the one called 'catnip'?"

Tau did not appear surprised at that demand—the Medic of a Free Trading spacer was never surprised at anything. He had his surfeit of shocks during his first years of service and after that accepted any occurrence, no matter how weird, as matter-of-fact. In addition Tau's hobby was "magic," the hidden knowledge possessed and used by witch doctors and medicine men on alien worlds. He had a library of recordings, of odd scraps of information, of certified results of certain very peculiar experiments. Now and then he wrote a report which was sent into Central Service, read with raised eyebrows by perhaps half a dozen incredulous desk warmers, and filed away to be safely forgotten. But even that had ceased to frustrate him.

"It's an herb of the mint family from Terra," he replied. "Mura grows it for Sinbad—has quite a marked influence on cats. Frank's been trying to keep him anchored to the ship by allowing him to roll in fresh leaves. He does it—then continues to sneak out whenever he can—"

That explained something for Dane—why the Salariki cub wished to enter the Queen tonight. Some of the scent of the plant had clung to Sinbad's fur, had been detected, and the Salarik had wanted to trace it to its source.

"Is it a drug?" Van Rycke prodded.

"In the way that all herbs are drugs. Human beings have dosed themselves in the past with a tea made of the dried leaves. It has no great medicinal properties. To felines it is a stimulation—and they get the same satisfaction from rolling in and eating the leaves as we do from drinking—"

"The Salariki are, in a manner of speaking, felines—" Van Rycke mused.

Tau straightened. "The Salariki have discovered catnip, I take it?"

Van Rycke nodded at Dane and for the second time the Cargo-master apprentice made his report. When he was done Van Rycke asked a direct question of the medical officer:

"What affect would catnip have on a Salarik?"

It was only then that Dane grasped the enormity of what he had done. They had no way of gauging the influence of an off-world plant on alien metabolism. What if he had introduced to the natives of Sargol a dangerous drug—started that cub on some path of addiction. He was cold inside Why, he might even have poisoned the child!

Tau picked up his cap, and after a second's hesitation, his emergency medical kit. He had only one question for Dane.

"Any idea of who the cub is—what clan he belongs to?"

And Dane, chill with real fear, was forced to answer in the negative. What *had* he done!

"Can you find him?" Van Rycke, ignoring Dane, spoke to Tau.

The Medic shrugged. "I can try. I was out scouting this morning—met one of the storm priests who handles their medical work. But I wasn't welcomed. However, under the circumstances, we have to try something—"

In the corridor Van Rycke had an order for Dane. "I suggest that you keep to quarters, Thorson, until we know how matters stand."

Dane saluted. That note in his superior's voice was like a whip lash—much worse to take than the abuse of a lesser man. He swallowed as he shut himself into his own cramped cubby. This might be the end of their venture. And they would be lucky if their charter was not withdrawn. Let I-S get an inkling of his rash action and the Company would have them up before the Board to be stripped of all their rights in the Service. Just because of his own stupidity—his pride in being able to break through where Van Rycke and the Captain had faced a stone wall. And, worse than the future which could face the Queen, was the thought that he might have introduced some dangerous drug into Sargol with his gift of those few leaves. When would he learn? He threw himself face down on his bunk and despondently pictured the string of calamities which could and maybe would stem from his thoughtless and hasty action.

Within the Queen night and day were mechanical—the lighting in the cabins did not vary much. Dane did not know how long he lay there forcing his mind to consider his stupid action, making himself face that in the Service there were no short cuts which endangered others—not unless those taking the risks were Terrans.

"Dane—!" Rip Shannon's voice cut through his self-imposed

nightmare. But he refused to answer. "Dane—Van wants you
on the double!"

Why? To bring him up before Jellico probably. Dane
schooled his expression, got up, pulling his tunic straight, still
unable to meet Rip's eyes. Shannon was just one of those he
had let down so badly. But the other did not notice his mood.
"Wait 'til you see them.—! Half Sargol must be here yell-
ing for trade!"

That comment was so far from what he had been expecting
that Dane was startled out of his own gloomy thoughts. Rip's
brown face was one wide smile, his black eyes danced—it was
plain he was honestly elated.

"Get a move on, fire rockets," he urged, "or Van will blast
you for fair!"

Dane did move, up the ladder to the next level and out on
the port ramp. What he saw below brought him up short.
Evening had come to Sargol but the scene immediately below
was not in darkness. Blazing torches advanced in lines from
the grass forest and the portable flood light of the spacer added
to the general glare, turning night into noonday.

Van Rycke and Jellico sat on stools facing at least five of the
seven major chieftains with whom they had conferred to no
purpose earlier. And behind these leaders milled a throng of
lesser Salariki. Yes, there was at least one carrying chair—and
also an orgel from the back of which a veiled noblewoman was
being assisted to dismount by two retainers. The women of the
clans were coming—which could mean only that trade was at
last in progress. But trade for what?

Dane strode down the ramp. He saw Paft, his hand carefully
covered by his trade cloth, advance to Van Rycke, whose own
fingers were decently veiled by a handkerchief. Under the folds
of fabric their hands touched. The bargaining was in the first
stages. And it was trading important enough for the clan leaders
to conduct themselves. Where, according to Cam's records, it
had been usual to delegate that power to a favored leige man.

Catching the light from the ship's beam and from the softer
flares of the Salariki torches was a small pile of stones resting

on a stool to one side. Dane drew a deep breath. He had heard the Koros stones described, had seen the tri-dee print of one found among Cam's recordings but the reality was beyond his expectations. He knew the technical analysis of the gems—that they were, as the amber of Terra, the fossilized resin exuded by ancient plants (maybe the ancestors of the grass trees) long buried in the saline deposits of the shallow seas where chemical changes had taken place to produce the wonder jewels. In color they shaded from a rosy apricot to a rich mauve, but in their depths other colors, silver, fiery gold, spun sparks which seemed to move as the gem was turned. And—which was what first endeared them to the Salariki—when worn against the skin and warmed by body heat they gave off a perfume which enchanted not only the Sargolian natives but all in the Galaxy wealthy enough to own one.

On another stool placed at Van Rycke's right hand, as that bearing the Koros stones was at Paft's, was a transparent plastic box containing some wrinkled brownish leaves. Dane moved as unobtrusively as he could to his proper place at such a trading session, behind Van Rycke. More Salariki were tramping out of the forest, torch bearing retainers and cloaked warriors. A little to one side was a third party Dane had not seen before.

They were clustered about a staff which had been driven into the ground, a staff topped with a white streamer marking a temporary trading ground. These were Salariki right enough but they did not wear the colorful garb of those about them, instead they were all clad alike in muffling, sleeved robes of a drab green—the storm priests—their robes denoting the color of the Sargolian sky just before the onslaught of their worst tempests. Cam had not left many clues concerning the religion of the Salariki, but the storm priests had, in narrowly defined limits, power, and their recognition of the Terran Traders would add to good feeling.

In the knot of storm priests a Terran stood—Medic Tau— and he was talking earnestly with the leader of the religious party. Dane would have given much to have been free to cross

and ask Tau a question or two. Was all this assembly the result
of the discovery in the hydro? But even as he asked himself
that, the trade cloths were shaken from the hands of the bar-
gainers and Van Rycke gave an order over his shoulder.

"Measure out two spoonsful of the dried leaves into a box—"
he pointed to a tiny plastic container.

With painstaking care Dane followed directions. At the same
time a servant of the Salarik chief swept the handful of gems
from the other stool and dropped them in a heap before Van
Rycke, who transferred them to a strong box resting between
his feet. Paft arose—but he had hardly quitted the trading
seat before one of the lesser clan leaders had taken his place,
the bargaining cloth ready looped loosely about his wrist.

It was at that point that the proceedings were interrupted.
A new party came into the open, their utilitarian Trade tunics
making a drab blot as they threaded their way in a compact
group through the throng of Salariki. I-S men! So they had not
lifted from Sargol.

They showed no signs of uneasiness—it was as if *their* rights
were being infringed by the Free Traders. And Kallee, their
Cargo-master, swaggered straight to the bargaining point. The
chatter of Salariki voices was stilled, the Sargolians withdrew
a little, letting one party of Terrans face the other, sensing
drama to come. Neither Van Rycke nor Jellico spoke, it was
left to Kallee to state his case.

"You've crooked your orbit this time, bright boys," his jeer
was a pean of triumph. "Code Three—Article six—or can't you
absorb rules tapes with you thick heads?"

Code Three—Article six, Dane searched his memory for that
law of the Service. The words flashed into his mind as the
auto-learner had planted them during his first year of training
back in the Pool.

" 'To no alien race shall any Trader introduce any drug, food,
or drink from off world, until such a substance has been certified as nonharmful to the aliens.' "

There it was! I-S had them and it was all his fault. But if he
had been so wrong, why in the world did Van Rycke sit there

trading, condoning the error and making it into a crime for which they could be summoned before the Board and struck off the rolls of the Service?

Van Rycke smiled gently. "Code Four—Article two," he quoted with the genial air of one playing gift-giver at a Forkidan feasting.

Code Four, Article two: Any organic substance offered for trade must be examined by a committee of trained medical experts, an equal representation of Terrans and aliens.

Kallee's sneering smile did not vanish. "Well," he challenged, "where's your board of experts?"

"Tau!" Van Rycke called to the Medic with the storm priests. "Will you ask your colleague to be so kind as to allow the Cargo-master Kallee to be presented?"

The tall, dark young Terran Medic spoke to the priest beside him and together they came across the clearing. Van Rycke and Jellico both arose and inclined their heads in honor to the priests, as did the chief with whom they had been about to deal.

"Reader of clouds and master of many winds," Tau's voice flowed with the many voweled titles of the Sargolian, "may I bring before your face Cargo-master Kallee, a servant of Inter-Solar in the realm of Trade?"

The storm priest's shaven skull and body gleamed steel gray in the light. His eyes, of that startling blue-green, regarded the I-S party with cynical detachment.

"You wish of me?" Plainly he was one who believed in getting down to essentials at once.

Kallee could not be overawed. "These Free Traders have introduced among your people a powerful drug which will bring much evil," he spoke slowly in simple words as if he were addressing a cub.

"You have evidence of such evil?" countered the storm priest. "In what manner is this new plant evil?"

For a moment Kallee was disconcerted. But he rallied quickly. "It has not been tested—you do not know how it will affect your people—"

The storm priest shook his head impatiently. "We are not lacking in intelligence, Trader. This plant *has* been tested, both by your master of life secrets and ours. There is no harm in it —rather it is a good thing, to be highly prized—so highly that we shall give thanks that it was brought unto us. This speech-together is finished." He pulled the loose folds of his robe closer about him and walked away.

"Now," Van Rycke addressed the I-S party, "I must ask you to withdraw. Under the rules of Trade your presence here can be actively resented—"

But Kallee had lost little of his assurance. "You haven't heard the last of this. A tape of the whole proceedings goes to the Board—"

"As you wish. But in the meantime—" Van Rycke gestured to the waiting Salariki who were beginning to mutter impatiently. Kallee glanced around, heard those mutters, and made the only move possible, away from the Queen. He was not quite so cocky, but neither had he surrendered.

Dane caught at Tau's sleeve and asked the question which had been burning in him since he had come upon the scene.

"What happened—about the catnip?"

There was lightening of the serious expression on Tau's face.

"Fortunately for you that child took the leaves to the storm priest. They tested and approved it. And I can't see that it has any ill effects. But you were just lucky, Thorson—it might have gone another way."

Dane sighed. "I know that, sir," he confessed. "I'm not trying to rocket out—"

Tau gave a half-smile. "We all off-fire our tubes at times," he conceded. "Only next time—"

He did not need to complete that warning as Dane caught him up:

"There isn't going to be a next time like this, sir—ever!"

chapter 4

GORP HUNT

But the interruption had disturbed the tenor of trading. The small chief who had so eagerly taken Paft's place had only two Koros stones to offer and even to Dane's inexperienced eyes they were inferior in size and color to those the other clan leader had tendered. The Terrans were aware that Koros mining was a dangerous business but they had not known that the stock of available stones was so very small. Within ten minutes the last of the serious bargaining was concluded and the clansmen were drifting away from the burned over space about the Queen's standing fins.

Dane folded up the bargain cloth, glad for a task. He sensed that he was far from being back in Van Rycke's good graces. The fact that his superior did not discuss any of the aspects of the deals with him was a bad sign.

Captain Jellico stretched. Although his was not, or never, what might be termed a good-humored face, he was at peace with his world. "That would seem to be all. What's the haul, Van?"

"Ten first class stones, about fifty second grade, and twenty or so of third. The chiefs will go to the fisheries tomorrow. *Then* we'll be in to see the really good stuff."

"And how's the herbs holding out?" That interested Dane too. Surely the few plants in the hydro and the dried leaves could not be stretched too far.

"As well as we could expect." Van Ryke frowned. "But Craig thinks he's on the trail of something to help—"

The storm priests had uprooted the staff marking the trading station and were wrapping the white streamer about it. Their leader had already gone and now Tau came up to the group by the ramp.

"Van says you have an idea," the Captain hailed him.

"We haven't tried it yet. And we can't unless the priests give it a clear lane—"

"That goes without saying—" Jellico agreed.

The Captain had not addressed that remark to him personally, but Dane was sure it had been directed at him. Well, they needn't worry—never again was he going to make that mistake, they could be very sure of that.

He was part of the conference which followed in the mess cabin only because he was a member of the crew. How far the reason for his disgrace had spread he had no way of telling, but he made no overtures, even to Rip.

Tau had the floor with Mura as an efficient lieutenant. He discussed the properties of catnip and gave information on the limited supply the Queen carried. Then he launched into a new suggestion.

"Felines of Terra, in fact a great many other of our native mammals, have a similiar affinity for this."

Mura produced a small flask and Tau opened it, passing it to Captain Jellico and so from hand to hand about the room. Each crewman sniffed at the strong aroma. It was a heavier scent than that given off by the crushed catnip—Dane was not sure he liked it. But a moment later Sinbad streaked in from the corridor and committed the unpardonable sin of leaping to the table top just before Mura who had taken the flask from

Dane. He miaowed plaintively and clawed at the steward's cuff. Mura stoppered the flask and put the cat down on the floor.

"What is it?" Jellico wanted to know.

"Anisette, a liquor made from the oil of anise—from seeds of the anise plant. It is a stimulant, but we use it mainly as a condiment. If it is harmless for the Salariki it ought to be a bigger bargaining point than any perfumes or spices, I-S can import. And remember, with their unlimited capital, they can flood the market with products we can't touch, selling at a loss if need be to cut us out. Because their ship is not going to lift from Sargol just because she has no legal right here."

"There's this point," Van Rycke added to the lecture. "The Eysies are trading or want to trade perfumes. But they stock only manufactured products, exotic stuff, but synthetic." He took from his belt pouch two tiny boxes.

Before he caught the rich scent of the paste inside them Dane had already identified each as luxury items from Casper —chemical products which sold well and at high prices in the civilized ports of the Galaxy. The Cargo-master turned the boxes over, exposing the symbol on their undersides—the mark of I-S.

"These were offered to me in trade by a Salarik. I took them, just to have proof that the Eysies are operating here. But— note—they were offered to me in trade, along with two top Koros for what? One spoonful of dried catnip leaves. Does that suggest anything?"

Mura answered first. "The Salariki prefer natural products to synthetic."

"I think so."

"D'you suppose that was Cam's secret?" speculated Astrogator Steen Wilcox.

"If it was," Jellico cut in, "he certainly kept it! If we had only known this earlier—"

They were all thinking of that, of their storage space carefully packed with useless trade goods. Where, if they had known, the same space could have carried herbs with five or twenty-five times as much buying power.

"Maybe now that their sales' resistance is broken, we *can* switch to some of the other stuff," Tang Ya, torn away from his beloved communicators for the conference, said wistfully. "They like color—how about breaking out some rolls of Harlinian moth silk?"

Van Rycke sighed wearily. "Oh, we'll try. We'll bring out everything and anything. But we could have done so much better—" he brooded over the tricks of fate which had landed them on a planet wild for trade with no proper trade goods in either of their holds.

There was a nervous little sound of a throat being apologetically cleared. Jasper Weeks, the small wiper from the engine room detail, the third generation Venusian colonist whom the more vocal members of the Queen's compliment were apt to forget upon occasion, seeing all eyes upon him, spoke though his voice was hardly above a hoarse whisper.

"Cedar—lacquel bark—forsh weed—"

"Cinnamon," Mura added to the list. "Imported in small quantities—"

"Naturally! Only the problem now is—how much cedar, lacquel bark, forsh weed, cinnamon do we have on board?" demanded Van Rycke.

His sarcasm did not register with Weeks for the little man pushed by Dane and left the cabin to their surprise. In the quiet which followed they could hear the clatter of his boots on ladder rungs as he descended to the quarters of the engine room staff. Tang turned to his neighbor, Johan Stotz, the Queen's Engineer.

"What's he going for?"

Stotz shrugged. Weeks was a self-effacing man—so much so that even in the cramped quarters of the spacer very little about him as an individual impressed his mates—a fact which was slowly dawning on them all now. Then they heard the scramble of feet hurrying back and Weeks burst in with energy which carried him across to the table behind which the Captain and Van Rycke now sat.

In the wiper's hands was a plasta-steel box—the treasure chest of a spaceman. Its tough exterior was guaranteed to protect the contents against everything but outright disintegration. Weeks put it down on the table and snapped up the lid.

A new aroma, or aromas, was added to the scents now at war in the cabin. Weeks pulled out a handful of fluffy white stuff which frothed up about his fingers like soap lather. Then with more care he lifted up a tray divided into many small compartments, each with a separate sealing lid of its own. The men of the Queen moved in, their curiosity aroused, until they were jostling one another.

Being tall Dane had an advantage, though Van Rycke's bulk and the wide shoulders of the Captain were between him and the object they were so intent upon. In each division of the tray, easily seen through the transparent lids, was a carved figure. The weird denizens of the Venusian polar swamps were there, along with life-like effigies of Terran animals, a Martian sand-mouse in all its monstrous ferocity, and the native animal and reptile life of half a hundred different worlds. Weeks put down a second tray beside the first, again displaying a menagerie of strange life forms. But when he clicked open one of the compartments and handed the figurine it contained to the Captain, Dane understood the reason for now bringing forward the carvings.

The majority of them were fashioned from a dull blue-gray wood and Dane knew that if he picked one up he would discover that it weighed close to nothing in his hand. That was lacquel bark—the aromatic product of a Venusian vine. And each little animal or reptile lay encased in a soft dab of frothy white—frosh weed—the perfumed seed casing of the Martian canal plants. One or two figures on the second tray were of a red-brown wood and these Van Rycke sniffed at appreciatively.

"Cedar—Terran cedar," he murmured.

Weeks nodded eagerly, his eyes alight. "I am waiting now for sandlewood—it is also good for carving—"

Jellico stared at the array in puzzled wonder. "You have made these?"

Being an amateur xenobiologist of no small standing himself, the shapes of the carvings more than the material from which they fashioned held his attention.

All those on board the Queen had their own hobbies. The monotony of voyaging through hyper-space had long ago impressed upon men the need for occupying both hands and mind during the sterile days while they were forced into close companionship with few duties to keep them alert. Jellico's cabin was papered with tri-dee pictures of the rare animals and alien creatures he had studied in their native haunts or of which he kept careful and painstaking records. Tau had his magic, Mura not only his plants but the delicate miniature landscapes he fashioned, to be imprisoned forever in the hearts of protecting plasta balls. But Weeks had never shown his work before and now he had an artist's supreme pleasure of completely confounding his shipmates.

The Cargo-master returned to the business on hand first. "You're willing to transfer these to 'cargo'?" he asked briskly. "How many do you have?"

Weeks, now lifting a third and then a fourth tray from the box, replied without looking up.

"Two hundred. Yes, I'll transfer, sir."

The Captain was turning about in his fingers the beautifully shaped figure of an Astran duocorn. "Pity to trade these here," he mused aloud. "Will Paft or Halfner appreciate more than just their scent?"

Weeks smiled shyly. "I've filled this case, sir. I was going to offer them to Mr. Van Rycke on a venture. I can always make another set. And right now—well, maybe they'll be worth more to the Queen, seeing as how they're made out of aromatic woods, then they'd be elsewhere. Leastwise the Eysies aren't going to have anything like them to show!" he ended in a burst of honest pride.

"Indeed they aren't!" Van Rycke gave honor where it was due.

So they made plans and then separated to sleep out the rest of the night. Dane knew that his lapse was not forgotten nor forgiven, but now he was honestly too tired to care and slept as well as if his conscience were clear.

But morning brought only a trickle of lower class clansmen for trading and none of them had much but news to offer. The storm priests, as neutral arbitrators, had divided up the Koros grounds. And the clansmen, under the personal supervision of their chieftains were busy hunting the stones. The Terrans gathered from scraps of information that gem seeking on such a large scale had never been attempted before.

Before night there came other news, and much more chilling. Paft, one of the two major chieftains of this section of Sargol —while supervising the efforts of his leige men on a newly discovered and richly strewn length of shoal water—had been attacked and killed by gorp. The unusual activity of the Salariki in the shallows had in turn drawn to the spot battalions of the intelligent, malignant reptiles who had struck in strength, slaying and escaping before the Salariki could form an adequate defense, having killed the land dwellers' sentries silently and effectively before advancing on the laboring main bodies of gem hunters.

A loss of a certain number of miners or fishers had been foreseen as the price one paid for Koros in quantity. But the death of a chieftain was another thing altogether, having repercussions which carried far beyond the fact of his death. When the news reached the Salariki about the Queen they melted away into the grass forest and for the first time the Terrans felt free of spying eyes.

"What happens now?" Ali inquired. "Do they declare all deals off?"

"That might just be the unfortunate answer," agreed Van Rycke.

"Could be," Rip commented to Dane, "that they'd think we were in someway responsible—"

But Dane's conscience, sensitive over the whole matter of Salariki trade, had already reached that conclusion.

The Terran party, unsure of what were the best tactics, wisely decided to do nothing at all for the time being. But, when the Salariki seemed to have completely vanished on the morning of the second day, the men were restless. Had Paft's death resulted in some inter-clan quarrel over the heirship and the other clans withdrawn to let the various contendents for that honor fight it out? Or—what was more probable and dangerous—had the aliens come to the point of view that the Queen was in the main responsible for the catastrophe and were engaged in preparing too warm a welcome for any Traders who dared to visit them?

With the latter idea in mind they did not stray far from the ship. And the limit of their traveling was the edge of the forest from which they could be covered and so they did not learn much.

It was well into the morning before they were dramatically appraised that, far from being considered in any way an enemy, they were about to be accepted in a tie as close as clan to clan during one of the temporary but binding truces.

The messenger came in state, a young Salarik warrior, his splendid cloak rent and hanging in tattered pieces from his shoulders as a sign of his official grief. He carried in one hand a burned out torch, and in the other an unsheathed claw knife, its blade reflecting the sunlight with a wicked glitter. Behind him trotted three couples of retainers, their cloaks also ragged fringes, their knives drawn.

Standing up on the ramp to receive what could only be a formal deputation were Captain, Astrogator, Cargo-master and Engineer, the senior officers of the spacer.

In the rolling periods of the Trade Lingo the torch bearer identified himself as Groft, son and heir of the late lamented Paft. Until his chieftain father was avenged in blood he could not assume the high seat of his clan nor the leadership of the family. And now, following custom, he was inviting the friends and sometime allies of the dead Paft to a gorp hunt. Such a gorp hunt, Dane gathered from amidst the flowers of ceremonial Salariki speech, as had never been planned before on the face of Sargol. Salariki without number in the past had died beneath the ripping talons of the water reptiles, but it was seldom that a chieftain had so fallen and his clan were firm in their determination to take a full blood price from the killers.

"—and so, sky lords," Groft brought his oration to a close, "we come to ask that you send your young men to this hunting so that they may know the joy of plunging knives into the scaled death and see the horned ones die bathed in their own vile blood!"

Dane needed no hint from the Queen's officers that this invitation was a sharp departure from custom. By joining with the natives in such a foray the Terrans were being admitted to kinship of a sort, cementing relations by a tie which the I-S, or any other interloper from off-world, would find hard to break. It was a piece of such excellent good fortune as they would not have dreamed of three days earlier.

Van Rycke replied, his voice properly sonorous, sounding out the rounded periods of the rolling tongue which they had all been taught during the voyage, using Cam's recordings. Yes, the Terrans would join with pleasure in so good and great a cause. They would lend the force of their arms to the defeat of all gorp they had the good fortune to meet. Groft need only name the hour for them to join him—

It was not needful, the young Salariki chieftain-to-be hastened to tell the Cargo-master, that the senior sky lords concern themselves in this matter. In fact it would be against custom, for it was meet that such a hunt be left to warriors of few years, that they might earn glory and be able to stand before the fires at the Naming as men. Therefore—the thumb claw of Groft was extended to its greatest length as he used it to single out the Terrans he had been eyeing—let this one, and that, and that, and the fourth be ready to join with the Salariki party an hour after nooning on this very day and they would indeed teach the slimy, treacherous lurkers in the depths a well needed lesson.

The Salarik's choice with one exception had unerringly fallen upon the youngest members of the crew, Ali, Rip, and Dane in that order. But his fourth addition had been Jasper Weeks. Perhaps because of his native pallor of skin and slightness of body the oiler had seemed, to the alien, to be younger than his years. At any rate Groft had made it very plain that he chose these men and Dane knew that the Queen's officers would raise no objection which might upset the delicate balance of favorable relations.

Van Rycke did ask for one concession which was reluctantly granted. He received permission for the spacer's men to carry their sleep rods. Though the Salariki, apparently for some reason of binding and hoary custom, were totally opposed to hunting their age-old enemy with anything other than their duelists' weapons of net and claw knife.

"Go along with them," Captain Jellico gave his final orders to the four, "as long as it doesn't mean your own necks—understand? On the other hand dead heroes have never helped to lift a ship. And these gorp are tough from all accounts. You'll just have to use your own judgment about springing your rods on them—" He looked distinctly unhappy at that thought.

Ali was grinning and little Weeks tightened his weapon belt with a touch of swagger he had never shown before. Rip was his usual soft voiced self, dependable as a rock and a good base for the rest of them—taking command without question as they marched off to join Groft's company.

chapter 5

THE PERILOUS SEAS

The gorp hunters straggled through the grass forest in family groups, and the Terrans saw that the enterprise had forced another uneasy truce upon the district, for there were representatives from more than just Paft's own clan. All the Salariki were young and the parties babbled together in excitement. It was plain that this hunt, staged upon a large scale, was not only a means of revenge upon a hated enemy but, also, a sporting event of outstanding prestige.

Now the grass trees began to show ragged gaps, open spaces between their clumps, until the forest was only scattered groups and the party the Terrans had joined walked along a trail cloaked in knee-high, yellow-red fern growth. Most of the Salariki carried unlit torches, some having four or five bundled together, as if gorp hunting must be done after nightfall. And it *was* fairly late in the afternoon before they topped a rise of ground and looked out upon one of Sargol's seas.

The water was a dull, metallic gray, broken by great swaths

of purple as if an artist had slapped a brush of color across it in a hit or miss fashion. Sand of the red grit, lightened by the golden flecks which glittered in the sun, stretched to the edge of the wavelets breaking with oily languor on the curve of earth. The bulk of islands arose in serried ranks farther out—crowned with grass trees all rippling under the sea wind.

They came out upon the beach where one of the purple patches touched the shore and Dane noted that it left a scummy deposit there. The Terrans went on to the water's edge. Where it was clear of the purple stuff they could get a murky glimpse of the bottom, but the scum hid long stretches of shoreline and outer wave, and Dane wondered if the gorp used it as a protective covering.

For the moment the Salariki made no move toward the sea which was to be their hunting ground. Instead the youngest members of the party, some of whom were adolescents not yet entitled to wear the claw knife of manhood, spread out along the shore and set industriously to gathering driftwood, which they brought back to heap on the sand. Dane, watching that harvest, caught sight of a smoothly polished length. He called Weeks' attention to the water rounded cylinder.

The oiler's eyes lighted and he stooped to pick it up. Where the other sticks were from grass trees this was something else. And among the bleached pile it had the vividness of flame. For it was a strident scarlet. Weeks turned it over in his hands, running his fingers lovingly across its perfect grain. Even in this crude state it had beauty. He stopped the Salarik who had just brought in another armload of wood.

"This is what?" he spoke the Trade Lingo haltingly.

The native gazed somewhat indifferently at the branch. "Tansil," he answered. "It grows on the islands—" He made a vague gesture to include a good section of the western sea before he hurried away.

Weeks now went along the tide line on his own quest, Dane trailing him. At the end of a quarter hour when a hail summoned them back to the site of the now lighted fire, they had some ten pieces of the tansil wood between them. The finds ranged from a three foot section some four inches in diameter, to some slender twigs no larger than a writing steelo—but all with high polish, the warm flame coloring. Weeks lashed them together before he joined the group where Groft was outlining the technique of gorp hunting for the benefit of the Terrans.

Some two hundred feet away a reef, often awash and stained with the purple scum, angled out into the sea in a long curve which formed a natural breakwater. This was the point of attack. But first the purple film must be removed so that land and sea dwellers could meet on common terms.

The fire blazed up, eating hungrily into the driftwood. And from it ran the young Salariki with lighted brands, which at the water's edge they whirled about their heads and then hurled out onto the purple patches. Fire arose from the water and ran with frantic speed across the crests of the low waves, while the Salariki coughed and buried their noses in their perfume boxes, for the wind drove shoreward an overpowering stench.

Where the cleansing fire had run on the water there was now only the natural metallic gray of the liquid, the cover was gone. Older Salariki warriors were choosing torches from those they had brought, doing it with care. Groft approached the Terrans carrying four.

"These you use now—"

What for? Dane wondered. The sky was still sunlit. He held the torch watching to see how the Salariki made use of them.

Groft led the advance—running lightly out along the reef with agile and graceful leaps to cross the breaks where the sea hurled in over the rock. And after him followed the other natives, each with a lighted torch in hand—the torch they hunkered down to plant firmly in some crevice of the rock before taking a stand beside that beacon.

The Terrans, less surefooted in the space boots, picked their way along the same path, wet with spray, wrinkling their noses against the lingering puffs of the stench from the water.

Following the example of the Salariki they faced seaward— but Dane did not know what to watch for. Cam had left only the vaguest general description of gorp and beyond the fact that they were reptilian, intelligent and dangerous, the Terrans had not been briefed.

Once the warriors had taken up their stand along the reef, the younger Salariki went into action once more. Lighting more torches at the fire, they ran out along the line of their elders and flung their torches as far as they could hurl them into the sea outside the reef.

The gray steel of the water was now yellow with the reflection of the sinking sun. But that ocher and gold became more brilliant yet as the torches of the Salariki set blazing up far floating patches of scum. Dane shielded his eyes against the glare and tried to watch the water, with some idea that this move must be provocation and what they hunted would so be driven into view.

He held his sleep rod ready, just as the Salarik on his right had claw knife in one hand and in the other, open and waiting, the net intended to entangle and hold fast a victim, binding him for the kill.

But it was at the far tip of the barrier—the post of greatest honor which Groft had jealously claimed as his, that the gorp struck first. At a wild shout of defiance Dane half turned to see the Salarik noble cast his net at sea level and then stab viciously with a well practiced blow. When he raised his arm for a second thrust, greenish ichor ran from the blade down his wrist.

"Dane!"

Thorson's head jerked around. He saw the vee of ripples headed straight for the rocks where he balanced. But he'd have to wait for a better target than a moving wedge of water. Instinctively he half crouched in the stance of an embattled spaceman, wishing now that he did have a blaster.

Neither of the Salariki stationed on either side of him made any move and he guessed that that was hunt etiquette. Each man was supposed to face and kill the monster that challenged him—without assistance. And upon his skill during the next few minutes might rest the reputation of all Terrans as far as the natives were concerned.

There was a shadow outline beneath the surface of the metallic water now, but he could not see well because of the distortion of the murky waves. He must wait until he was sure.

Then the thing gave a spurt and, only inches beyond the toes of his boots, a nightmare creature sprang half-way out of the water, pincher claws as long as his own arms snapping at him. Without being conscious of his act, he pressed the stud of the sleep rod, aiming in the general direction of that horror from the sea.

But to his utter amazement the creature did not fall supinely back into watery world from which it had emerged. Instead those claws snapped again, this time scrapping across the top of Dane's boot, leaving a furrow in material the keenest of knives could not have scored.

"Give it to him!" That was Rip shouting encouragement from his own place farther along the reef.

Dane pressed the firing stud again and again. The claws waved as the monstrosity slavered from a gaping frog's mouth, a mouth which was fanged with a shark's vicious teeth. It was almost wholly out of the water, creeping on a crab's many legs, with the clawed upper limbs reaching for him, when suddenly it stopped, its huge head turning from side to side in the sheltering carapace of scaled natural armor. It settled back as if crouching for a final spring—a spring which would push Dane into the ocean.

But that attack never came. Instead the gorp drew in upon itself until it resembled an unwieldy ball of indestructible armor and there it remained.

The Salariki on either side of Dane let out cries of triumph and edged closer. One of them twirled his net suggestively, seeing that the Terran lacked what was to him an essential piece of hunting equipment. Dane nodded vigorously in agreement and the tough strands swung out in a skillful cast which engulfed the motionless creature on the reef. But it was so protected by its scales that there was no opening for the claw knife. They had made a capture but they could not make a kill.

However the Salariki were highly delighted. And several abandoned their posts to help the boys drag the monster ashore where it was pinned down to the beach by stakes driven through the edges of the net.

But the hunting party was given little time to gloat over this stroke of fortune. The gorp killed by Groft and the one stunned by Dane were only the van of an army and within moments the hunters on the reef were confronted by trouble armed with slashing claws and diabolic fighting ability.

The battle was anything but one-sided. Dane whirled, as the air was rent by a shriek of agony, just in time to see one of the Salariki, already torn by the claws of a gorp, being drawn under the water. It was too late to save the hunter, though Dane, balanced on the very edge of the reef, aimed a beam into the bloody waves. If the gorp was affected by this attack he could not tell, for both attacker and victim could no longer be seen.

But Ali had better luck in rescuing the Salarik who shared his particular section of reef, and the native, gashed and spurting blood from a wound in his thigh, was hauled to safety. While the gorp, coiling too slowly under the Terran ray, was literally hewn to pieces by the revengeful knives of the hunter's kin.

The fight broke into a series of individual duels carried on now by the light of the torches as the evening closed in. The last of the purple patches had burned away to nothing. Dane crouched by his standard torch, his eyes fastened on the sea, watching for an ominous vee of ripples betraying another gorp on its way to launch against the rock barrier.

There was such wild confusion along that line of water sprayed rocks that he had no idea of how the engagement was going. But so far the gorp showed no signs of having had enough.

Dane was shaken out of his absorption by another scream. One, he was sure, which had not come from any Salariki throat. He got to his feet. Rip was stationed four men beyond him. Yes, the tall Astrogator-apprentice was there, outlined against torch flare. Ali? No—there was the assistant Engineer. Weeks? But Weeks was picking his way back along the reef toward the shore, haste expressed in every line of his figure. The scream sounded for a second time, freezing the Terrans.

"Come back—!" That was Weeks gesturing violently at the shore and something floundering in the protecting circle of the reef. The younger Salariki who had been feeding the fire were now clustered at the water's edge.

Ali ran and with a leap covered the last few feet, landing recklessly knee deep in the waves. Dane saw light strike on his rod as he swung it in a wide arc to center on the struggle churning the water into foam. A third scream died to a moan and then the Salariki dashed into the sea, their nets spread, drawing back with them through the surf a dark and now quiet mass.

The fact that at least one gorp had managed to get on the inner side of the reef made an impression on the rest of the native hunters. After an uncertain minute or two Groft gave the signal to withdraw—which they did with grisly trophies. Dane counted seven gorp bodies—which did not include the prisoner ashore. And more might have slid into the sea to die. On the other hand two Salariki were dead—one had been drawn into the sea before Dane's eyes—and at least one was badly wounded. But who had been pulled down in the shallows —some one sent out from the Queen with a message?

Dane raced back along the reef, not waiting to pull up his torch, and before he reached the shore Rip was overtaking him. But the man who lay groaning on the sand was not from the Queen. The torn and bloodstained tunic covering his lacerated shoulders had the I-S badge. Ali was already at work on his wounds, giving temporary first aid from his belt kit. To all their questions he was stubbornly silent—either he couldn't or wouldn't answer.

In the end they helped the Salariki rig three stretchers. On one, the largest, the captive gorp, still curled in a round carapace protected ball, was bound with the net. The second supported the wounded Salarik clansman and onto the third the Terrans lifted the I-S man.

"We'll deliver him to his own ship," Rip decided. "He must have tailed us here as a spy—" He asked a passing Salarik as to where they could find the Company spacer.

"They might just think we are responsible," Ali pointed out. "But I see your point. If we do pack him back to the Queen and he doesn't make it, they might say that we fired his rockets for him. All right, boys, let's up-ship—he doesn't look too good to me."

With a torch-bearing Salarik boy as a guide, they hurried along a path taking in turns the burden of the stretcher. Luckily the I-S ship was even closer to the sea than the Queen and as they crossed the slagged ground, congealed by the break fire, they were trotting.

Though the Company ship was probably one of the smallest Inter-Solar carried on her rosters, it was a third again as large as the Queen—with part of that third undoubtedly dedicated to extra cargo space. Beside her their own spacer would seem not only smaller, but battered and worn. But no Free Trader would have willingly assumed the badges of a Company man, not even for the command of such a ship fresh from the cradles of a builder.

When a man went up from the training Pool for his first assignment, he was sent to the ship where his temperament, training and abilities best fitted. And those who were designated as Free Traders could never fit into the pattern of Company men. Of late years the breech between those who lived under the strict parental control of one of the five great galaxy wide organizations and those still too much of an individual to live any life but that of the half-explorer-half-pioneer which was the Free Trader's, had widened alarmingly. Antagonism flared, rivalry was strong. But as yet the great Companies themselves were at polite cold war with one another for the big plums of the scattered systems. The Free Traders took the crumbs and there was not much disputing—save in cases such as had arisen on Sargol, when suddenly crumbs assumed the guise of very rich cake, rich and large enough to attract a giant.

The party from the Queen was given a peremptory challenge as they reached the other ship's ramp. Rip demanded to see the officer of the watch and then told the story of the wounded man as far as they knew it. The Eysie was hurried aboard—nor did his shipmates give a word of thanks.

"That's that." Rip shrugged. "Let's go before they slam the hatch so hard they'll rock their ship off her fins!"

"Polite, aren't they?" asked Weeks mildly.

"What do you expect of Eysies?" Ali wanted to know. "To them Free Traders are just rim planet trash. Let's report back where we are appreciated."

They took a short cut which brought them back to the Queen and they filed up her ramp to make their report to the Captain.

But they were not yet finished with Groft and his gorp slayers. No Salarik appeared for trade in the morning—surprising the Terrans. Instead a second delegation, this time of older men and a storm priest, visited the spacer with an invitation to attend Paft's funeral feast, a rite which would be followed by the formal elevation of Groft to his father's position, now that he had revenged that parent. And from remarks dropped by members of the delegation it was plain that the bearing of the Terrans who had joined the hunting party was esteemed to have been in highest accord with Salariki tradition.

They drew lots to decide which two must remain with the ship and the rest perfumed themselves so as to give no offence which might upset their now cordial relations. Again it was mid-afternoon when the Salariki escort sent to do them honor waited at the edge of the wood and Mura and Tang saw them off. With a herald booming before them, they traveled the beaten earth road in the opposite direction from the trading center, off through the forest until they came to a wide section of several miles which had been rigorously cleared of any vegetation which might give cover to a lurking enemy. In the center of this was a twelve-foot-high stockade of the bright red, burnished wood which had attracted Weeks on the shore. Each paling was the trunk of a tree and it had been sharpened at the top to a wicked point. On the field side was a wide ditch, crossed at the gate by a bridge, the planking of which might be removed at will. And as Dane passed over he looked down into a moat that was dry. The Salariki did not depend upon water for a defense—but on something else which his experience of the previous night had taught him to respect. There was no mistaking that shade of purple. The highly inflammable scum the hunters had burnt from the top of the waves had been brought inland and lay a greasy blanket some eight feet below. It would only be necessary to toss a torch on that and the defenders of the stockade would create a wall of fire to baffle any attacker. The Salariki knew how to make the most of their world's natural resources.

chapter 6

DUELIST'S CHALLENGE

Inside the red stockade there was a crowded community. The Salariki demanded privacy of a kind, and even the unmarried warriors did not share barracks, but each had a small cubicle of his own. So that the mud brick and timber erections of one of their clan cities resembled nothing so much as the comb cells of a busy beehive. Although Paft's was considered a large clan, it numbered only about two hundred fighting men and their numerous wives, children and captive servants. Not all of them normally lived at this center, but for the funeral feasting they had assembled—which meant a lot of doubling up and tenting out under makeshift cover between the regular buildings of the town. So that the Terrans were glad to be guided through this crowded maze to the Great Hall which was its heart.

As the trading center had been, the hall was a circular enclosure open to the sky above but divided in wheel-spoke fashion with posts of the red wood, each supporting a metal basket filled with inflammable material. Here were no lowly stools or trading tables. One vast circular board, broken only by a gap at the foot, ran completely around the wall. At the end opposite the entrance was the high chair of the chieftain, set on a two step dais. Though the feast had not yet officially begun, the Terrans saw that the majority of the places were already occupied.

They were led around the perimeter of the enclosure to places not far from the high seat. Van Rycke settled down with a grunt of satisfaction. It was plain that the Free Traders were numbered among the nobility. They could be sure of good trade in the days to come.

Delegations from neighboring clans arrived in close companies of ten or twelve and were granted seats, as had been the Terrans, in groups. Dane noted that there was no intermingling of clan with clan. And, as they were to understand later that night, there was a very good reason for that precaution.

"Hope all our adaption shots work," Ali murmured, eyeing with no pleasure at all the succession of platters now being borne through the inner opening of the table.

While the Traders had learned long ago that the wisest part of valor was not to sample alien strong drinks, ceremony often required that they break bread (or its other world equivalent) on strange planets. And so science served expediency and now a Trader bound for any Galactic banquet was immunized, as far as was medically possible, against the evil consequences of consuming food not originally intended for Terran stomachs. One of the results being that Traders acquired a far flung reputation of possessing bird-like appetites—since it was always better to nibble and live, than to gorge and die.

Groft had not yet taken his place in the vacant chieftain's chair. For the present he stood in the center of the table circle, directing the captive slaves who circulated with the food. Until the magic moment when the clan themselves would proclaim him their overlord, he remained merely the eldest son of the house, relatively without power.

As the endless rows of platters made their way about the table the basket lights on the tops of the pillars were ignited, dispelling the dusk of evening. And there was an attendant stationed by each to throw on handsful of aromatic bark which burned with puffs of lavender smoke, adding to the many warring scents. The Terrans had recourse at intervals to their own pungent smelling bottles, merely to clear their heads of the drugging fumes.

Luckily, Dane thought as the feast proceeded, that smoke from the braziers went straight up. Had they been in a roofed space they might have been overcome. As it was—were they entirely conscious of all that was going on around them?

His reason for that speculation was the dance now being performed in the center of the hall—their fight with the gorp being enacted in a series of bounds and stabbings. He was sure that he could no longer trust his eyes when the claw knife of the victorious dancer-hunter apparently passed completely through the chest of another wearing a grotesque monster mask.

As a fitting climax to their horrific display, three of the men who had been with them on the reef entered, dragging behind them—still enmeshed in the hunting net—the gorp which Dane had stunned. It was uncurled now and very much alive, but the pincer claws which might have cut its way to safety were encased in balls of hard substance.

Freed from the net, suspended by its sealed claws, the gorp swung back and forth from a standard set up before the high seat. Its murderous jaws snapped futilely, and from it came an enraged snake's vicious hissing. Though totally in the power of its enemies it gave an impression of terrifying strength and menace.

The sight of their ancient foe aroused the Salariki, inflaming warriors who leaned across the table to hurl tongue-twisting invective at the captive monster. Dane gathered that seldom had a living gorp been delivered helpless into their hands and they proposed to make the most of this wonderful opportunity. And the Terran suddenly wished that the monstrosity had fallen back into the sea. He had no soft thoughts for the gorp after what he had seen at the reef and the tales he had heard, but neither did he like what he saw now expressed in gestures, heard in the tones of voices about them.

A storm priest put an end to the outcries. His dun cloak making a spot of darkness amid all the flashing color, he came straight to the place where the gorp swung. As he took his stand before the wriggling creature the din gradually faded, the warriors settled back into their seats, a pool of quiet spread through the enclosure.

Groft came up to take his position beside the priest. With both hands he carried a two handled cup. It was not the ornamented goblet which stood before each diner, but a manifestly older artifact, fashioned of some dull black substance and having the appearance of being even older than the hall or town.

One of the warriors who had helped to bring in the gorp now made a quick and accurate cast with a looped rope, snaring the monster's head and pulling back almost at a right angle. With deliberation the storm priest produced a knife—the first straight bladed weapon Dane had seen on Sargol. He made a single thrust in the soft underpart of the gorp's throat, catching in the cup he took from Groft some of the ichor which spurted from the wound.

The gorp thrashed madly, spattering table and surrounding Salariki with its life fluid, but the attention of the crowd was riveted elsewhere. Into the old cup the priest poured another substance from a flask brought by an underling. He shook the cup back and forth, as if to mix its contents thoroughly and then handed it to Groft.

Holding it before him the young chieftain leaped to the table top and so to a stand before the high seat. There was a hush throughout the enclosure. Now even the gorp had ceased its wild struggles and hung limp in its bonds.

Groft raised the cup above his head and gave a loud shout in the archaic language of his clan. He was answered by a chant from the warriors who would in battle follow his banner, a chant punctuated with the clinking slap of knife blades brought down forcibly on the board.

Three times he recited some formula and was answered by the others. Then, in another period of sudden quiet, he raised the cup to his lips and drank off its contents in a single draught, turning the goblet upside down when he had done to prove that not a drop remained within. A shout tore through the great hall. The Salariki were all on their feet, waving their knives over their heads in honor to their new ruler. And Groft for the first time seated himself in the high seat. The clan was no longer without a chieftain, Groft held his father's place.

"Show over?" Dane heard Stotz murmur and Van Rycke's disappointing reply:

"Not yet. They'll probably make a night of it. Here comes another round of drinks—"

"And trouble with them," that was Captain Jellico being prophetic.

"By the Coalsack's Ripcord!" That exclamation had been jolted out of Rip and Dane turned to see what had so jarred the usually serene Astrogator-apprentice. He was just in time to witness an important piece of Saroglian social practice.

A young warrior, surely only within a year or so of receiving his knife, was facing an older Salarik, both on their feet. The head and shoulder fur of the older fighter was dripping wet and an empty goblet rolled across the table to bump to the floor. A hush had fallen on the immediate neighbors of the pair, and there was an air of expectancy about the company.

"Threw his drink all over the other fellow," Rip's soft whisper explained. "That means a duel—"

"Here and now?" Dane had heard of the personal combat proclivities of the Salariki.

"Should be to the death for an insult such as that," Ali remarked, as usual surveying the scene from his chosen role as bystander. As a child he had survived the unspeakable massacres of the Crater War, nothing had been able to crack his surface armor since.

"The young fool!" that was Steen Wilcox sizing up the situation from the angle of a naturally cautious nature and some fifteen years of experience on a great many different worlds. "He'll be mustered out for good before he knows what happened to him!"

The younger Salarik had barked a question at his elder and

had been promptly answered by that dripping warrior. Now
their neighbors came to life with an efficiency which suggested
that they had been waiting for such a move, it had happened
so many times that every man knew just the right procedure
from that point on.

In order for a Sargolian‹ feast to be a success, the Terrans
gathered from overheard remarks, at least one duel must be
staged sometime during the festivities. And those not actively
engaged did a lost of brisk betting in the background.

"Look there—at that fellow in the violet cloak," Rip directed
Dane. "See what he just laid down?"

The nobleman in the violet cloak was not one of Groft's
liege men, but a member of a delegation from another clan.
And what he had laid down on the table—indicating as he did
so his choice as winner in the coming combat, the elder warrior—was a small piece of white material on which reposed a
slightly withered but familiar leaf. The neighbor he wagered
with, eyed the stake narrowly, bending over to sniff at it, before
he piled up two gem set armlets, a personal scent box and a
thumb ring to balance.

At this practical indication of just how much the Terran
herb was esteemed Dane regretted anew their earlier ignorance.
He glanced along the board and saw that Van Rycke had noted
that stake and was calling their Captain's attention to it.

But such side issues were forgotten as the duelists vaulted
into the circle rimmed by the table, a space now vacated for
their action. They were stripped to their loin cloths, their
cloaks thrown aside. Each carried his net in his right hand, his
claw knife ready in his left. As yet the Traders had not seen
Salarik against Salarik in action and in spite of themselves they
edged forward in their seats, as intent as the natives upon what
was to come. The finer points of the combat were lost on them,
and they did not understand the drilled casts of the net, which
had become as formalized through the centuries as the ancient
and now almost forgotten sword play of their own world. The
young Salarik had greater agility and speed, but the veteran who
faced him had the experience.

To Terran eyes the duel had some of the weaving, sweeping movements of the earlier ritual dance. The swift evasions of the nets were graceful and so timed that many times the meshes grazed the skin of the fighter who fled entrapment.

Dane believed that the elder man was tiring, and the youngster must have shared that opinion. There was a leap to the right, a sudden flurry of dart and retreat, and then a net curled high and fell, enfolding flailing arms and kicking legs. When the clutch rope was jerked tight, the captured youth was thrown off balance. He rolled frenziedly, but there was no escaping the imprisoning strands.

A shout applauded the victor. He stood now above his captive who lay supine, his throat or breast ready for either stroke of the knife his captor wished to deliver. But it appeared that the winner was not minded to end the encounter with blood. Instead he reached out a long, be-furred arm, took up a filled goblet from the table and with serious deliberation, poured its contents onto the upturned face of the loser.

For a moment there was a dead silence around the feast board and then a second roar, to which the honestly relieved Terrans added spurts of laughter. The sputtering youth was shaken free of the net and went down on his knees, tendering his opponent his knife, which the other thrust along with his own into his sash belt. Dane gathered from overheard remarks that the younger man was, for a period of time, to be determined by clan council, now the servant-slave of his overthrower and that since they were closely united by blood ties, this solution was considered eminently suitable—though had the elder killed his opponent, no one would have thought the worse of him for that deed.

It was the Queen's men who were to provide the next center of attraction. Groft climbed down from his high seat and came to face across the board those who had accompanied him on the hunt. This time there was no escaping the sipping of the potent drink which the new chieftain slopped from his own goblet into each of theirs.

The fiery mouthful almost gagged Dane, but he swallowed

manfully and hoped for the best as it burned like acid down his throat into his middle, there to mix uncomfortably with the viands he had eaten. Weeks' thin face looked very white, and Dane noticed with malicious enjoyment, that Ali had an unobtrusive grip on the table which made his knuckles stand out in polished knobs—proving that there *were* things which could upset the imperturbable Kamil.

Fortunately they were *not* required to empty that flowing bowl in one gulp as Groft had done. The ceremonial mouthful was deemed enough and Dane sat down thankfully—but with uneasy fears for the future.

Groft had started back to his high seat when there was an interruption which had not been foreseen. A messenger threaded his way among the serving men and spoke to the chieftain, who glanced at the Terrans and then nodded.

Dane, his queasiness growing every second, was not attending until he heard a bitten off word from Rip's direction and looked up to see a party of I-S men coming into the open space before the high seat. The men from the Queen stiffened—there was something in the attitude of the newcomers which hinted at trouble.

"What do you wish, sky lords?" That was Groft using the Trade Lingo, his eyes half closed as he lolled in his chair of state, almost as if he were about to witness some entertainment provided for his pleasure.

"We wish to offer you the good fortune desires of our hearts—" That was Kallee, the flowery words rolling with the proper accent from his tongue. "And that you shall not forget us—we also offer gifts—"

At a gesture from their Cargo-master, the I-S men set down a small chest. Groft, his chin resting on a clenched fist, lost none of his lazy air.

"They are received," he retorted with the formal acceptance. "And no one can have too much good fortune. The Howlers of the Black Winds know that." But he tendered no invitation to join the feast.

Kallee did not appear to be disconcerted. His next move was

one which took his rivals by surprise, in spite of their suspicions.

"Under the laws of the Fellowship, O, Groft," he clung to the formal speech, "I claim redress—"

Ali's hand moved. Through his growing distress Dane saw Van Rycke's jaw tighten, the fighting mask snap back on Captain Jellico's face. Whatever came now was real trouble.

Groft's eyes flickered over the party from the Queen. Though he had just pledged cup friendship with four of them, he had the malicious humor of his race. He would make no move to head off what might be coming.

"By the right of the knife and the net," he intoned, "you have the power to claim personal satisfaction. Where is your enemy?"

Kallee turned to face the Free Traders. "I hereby challenge a champion to be set out from these off-worlders to meet by the blood and by the water my champion—"

The Salariki were getting excited. This was superb entertainment, an engagement such as they had never hoped to see— alien against alien. The rising murmur of their voices was like the growl of a hunting beast.

Groft smiled and the pleasure that expression displayed was neither Terran—nor human. But then the clan leader was not either, Dane reminded himself.

"Four of these warriors are clan-bound," he said. "But the others may produce a champion—"

Dane looked along the line of his comrades—Ali, Rip, Weeks and himself had just been ruled out. That left Jellico, Van Rycke, Karl Kosti, the giant jetman whose strength they had had to rely upon before, Stotz the Engineer, Medic Tau and Steen Wilcox. If it were strength alone he would have chosen Kosti, but the big man was not too quick a thinker—

Jellico got to his feet, the embodiment of a star lane fighting man. In the flickering light the scar on his cheek seemed to ripple. "Who's your champion?" he asked Kallee.

The Eysie Cargo-master was grinning. He was confident he

had pushed them into a position from which they could not extricate themselves.

"You accept challenge?" he countered.

Jellico merely repeated his question and Kallee beckoned forward one of his men.

The Eysie who stepped up was no match for Kosti. He was a slender, almost wand-slim young man, whose pleased smirk said that he, too, was about to put something over on the notorious Free Traders. Jellico studied him for a couple of long seconds during which the hum of Salariki voices was the threatening buzz of a disturbed wasps' nest. There was no way out of this—to refuse conflict was to lose all they had won with the clansmen. And they did not doubt that Kallee had, in some way, triggered the scales against them.

Jellico made the best of it. "We accept challenge," his voice was level. "We, being guesting in Groft's holding, will fight after the manner of the Salariki who are proven warriors—" He paused as roars of pleased acknowledgment arose around the board.

"Therefore let us follow the custom of warriors and take up the net and the knife—"

Was there a shade of dismay on Kallee's face?

"And the time?" Groft leaned forward to ask—but his satisfaction at such a fine ending for his feast was apparent. This would be talked over by every Sargolian for many storm seasons to come!

Jellico glanced up at the sky. "Say an hour after dawn, chieftain. With your leave, we shall confer concerning a champion."

"My council room is yours," Groft signed for a liege man to guide them.

chapter 7

BARRING ACCIDENT

The morning winds rustled through the grass forest and, closer to hand, it pulled at the cloaks of the Salariki. Clan nobles sat on stools, lesser folk squatted on the trampled stubble of the cleared ground outside the stockade. In their many colored splendor the drab tunics of the Terrans were a blot of darkness at either end of the makeshift arena which had been marked out for them.

At the conclusion of their conference the Queen's men had been forced into a course Jellico had urged from the first. He, and he alone, would represent the Free Traders in the coming duel. And now he stood there in the early morning, stripped down to shorts and boots, wearing nothing on which a net could catch and so trap him. The Free Traders were certain that the I-S men having any advantage would press it to the ultimate limit and the death of Captain Jellico would make a great impression on the Salariki.

Jellico was taller than the Eysie who faced him, but almost

as lean. Hard muscles moved under his skin, pale where space tan had not burned in the years of his star voyaging. And his every movement was with the liquid grace of a man who, in his time, had been a master of the force blade. Now he gripped in his left hand the claw knife given him by Groft himself and in the other he looped the throwing rope of the net.

At the other end of the field, the Eysie man was industriously moving his bootsoles back and forth across the ground, intent upon coating them with as much of the gritty sand as would adhere. And he displayed the supreme confidence in himself which he had shown at the moment of challenge in the Great Hall.

None of the Free Trading party made the mistake of trying to give Jellico advice. The Captain had not risen to his command without learning his duties. And the duties of a Free Trader covered a wide range of knowledge and practice. One had to be equally expert with a blaster and a slingshot when the occasion demanded. Though Jellico had not fought a Salariki duel with net and knife before, he had a deep memory of other weapons, other tactics which could be drawn upon and adapted to his present need.

There was none of the casual atmosphere which had surrounded the affair between the Salariki clansmen in the hall. Here was ceremony. The storm priests invoked their own particular grim Providence, and there was an oath taken over the weapons of battle. When the actual engagement began the betting among the spectators had reached, Dane decided, epic proportions. Large sections of Sargolian personal property were due to change hands as a result of this encounter.

As the chief priest gave the order to engage both Terrans advanced from their respective ends of the fighting space with the half crouching, light footed tread of spacemen. Jellico had pulled his net into as close a resemblance to a rope as its bulk would allow. The very type of weapon, so far removed from any the Traders knew, made it a disadvantage rather than an asset.

But it was when the Eysie moved out to meet the Captain

that Rip's fingers closed about Dane's upper arm in an almost paralyzing grip.

"He knows—"

Dane had not needed that bad news to be made vocal. Having seen the exploits of the Salariki duelists earlier, he had already caught the significance of that glide, of the way the I-S champion carried his net. The Eysie had not had any last minute instruction in the use of Sargolian weapons—he had practiced and, by his stance, knew enough to make him a formidable menace. The clamor about the Queen's party rose as the battle-wise eyes of the clansmen noted that and the odds against Jellico reached fantastic heights while the hearts of his crew sank.

Only Van Rycke was not disturbed. Now and then he raised his smelling bottle to his nose with an elegant gesture which matched those of the befurred nobility around him, as if not a thought of care ruffled his mind.

The Eysie feinted in an opening which was a rather ragged copy of the young Salarik's more fluid moves some hours before. But, when the net settled, Jellico was simply not there, his quick drop to one knee had sent the mesh flailing in an arc over his bowed shoulders with a good six inches to spare. And a cry of approval came not only from his comrades, but from those natives who had been gamblers enough to venture their wagers on his performance.

Dane watched the field and the fighters through a watery film. The discomfort he had experienced since downing that mouthful of the cup of friendship had tightened into a fist of pain clutching his middle in a torturing grip. But he knew he must stick it out until Jellico's ordeal was over. Someone stumbled against him and he glanced up to see Ali's face, a horrible gray-green under the tan, close to his own. For a moment the Engineer-apprentice caught at his arm for support and then with a visible effort straightened up. So he wasn't the only one— He looked for Rip and Weeks and saw that they, too, were ill.

But for the moment all that mattered was the stretch of

trampled earth and the two men facing each other. The Eysie made another cast and this time, although Jellico was not caught, the slap of the mesh raised a red welt on his forearm. So far the Captain had been content to play the defensive role of retreat, studying his enemy, planning ahead.

The Eysie plainly thought the game his, that he had only to wait for a favorable moment and cinch the victory. Dane began to think it had gone on for weary hours. And he was dimly aware that the Salariki were also restless. One or two shouted angrily at Jellico in their own tongue.

The end came suddenly. Jellico lost his footing, stumbled, and went down. But before his men could move, the Eysie champion bounded forward, his net whirling out. Only he never reached the Captain. In the very act of falling Jellico had pulled his legs under him so that he was not supine but crouched, and his net swept out at ground level, clipping the I-S man about the shins, entangling his feet so that he crashed heavily to the sod and lay still.

"The whip—that Lalox whip trick!" Wilcox's voice rose triumphantly above the babble of the crowd. Using his net as if it had been a thong, Jellico had brought down the Eysie with a move the other had not foreseen.

Breathing hard, sweat running down his shoulders and making tracks through the powdery red dust which streaked him, Jellico got to his feet and walked over to the I-S champion who had not moved or made a sound since his fall. The Captain went down on one knee to examine him.

"Kill! Kill!" That was the Salariki, all their instinctive savagery aroused.

But Jellico spoke to Groft. "By our customs we do not kill the conquered. Let his friends bear him hence." He took the claw knife the Eysie still clutched in his hand and thrust it into his own belt. Then he faced the I-S party and Kallee.

"Take your man and get out!" The rein he had kept on his temper these past days was growing very thin. "You've made your last play here."

Kallee's thick lips drew back in something close to a Salarik snarl. But neither he nor his men made any reply. They bundled up their unconscious fighter and disappeared.

Of their own return to the sanctuary of the Queen Dane had only the dimmest of memories afterwards. He had made the privacy of the forest road before he yielded to the demands of his outraged interior. And after that he had stumbled along with Van Rycke's hand under his arm, knowing from other miserable sounds that he was not alone in his torment.

It was some time later, months he thought when he first roused, that he found himself lying in his bunk, feeling very weak and empty as if a large section of his middle had been removed, but also at peace with his world. As he levered himself up the cabin had a nasty tendency to move slowly to the right as if he were a pivot on which it swung, and he had all the sensations of being in free fall though the Queen was still firmly planeted. But that was only a minor discomfort compared to the disturbance he remembered.

Fed the semi-liquid diet prescribed by Tau and served up by Mura to him and his fellow sufferers, he speedily got back his strength. But it had been a close call, he did not need Tau's explanation to underline that. Weeks had suffered the least of the four, he the most—though none of them had had an easy time. And they had been out of circulation three days.

"The Eysie blasted last night," Rip informed him as they lounged in the sun on the ramp, sharing the blessed lazy hours of invalidism.

But somehow that news gave Dane no lift of spirit. "I didn't think they'd give up—"

Rip shrugged. "They may be off to make a dust-off before the Board. Only, thanks to Van and the Old Man, we're covered all along the line. There's nothing they can use against us to break our contract. And now we're in so solid they can't cut us out with the Salariki. Groft asked the Captain to teach him that trick with the net. I didn't know the Old Man knew Lalox whip fighting—it's about one of the nastiest ways to get cut to pieces in this universe—"

"How's trade going?"

Rip's sunniness clouded. "Supplies have given out. Weeks had an idea—but it won't bring in Koros. That red wood he's so mad about, he's persuaded Van to stow some in the cargo holds since we have enough Koros stones to cover the voyage. Luckily the clansmen will take ordinary trade goods in exchange for that and Weeks thinks it will sell on Terra. It's tough enough to turn a steel knife blade and yet it is light and easy to handle when it's cured. Queer stuff and the color's interesting. That stockade of it planted around Groft's town has been up close to a hundred years and not a sign of rot in a log of it!"

"Where is Van?"

"The storm priests sent for him. Some kind of a gabble-fest on the star-star level, I gather. Otherwise we're almost ready to blast. And we know what kind of a cargo to bring next time."

They certainly did, Dane agreed. But he was not to idle away his morning. An hour later a caravan came out of the forest, a line of complaining, burdened orgels, their tiny heads hanging low as they moaned their woes, the hard life which sent them on their sluggish way with piles of red logs lashed to their broad toads' backs. Weeks was in charge of the procession and Dane went to work with the cargo plan Van had left, seeing that the brilliant scarlet lengths were hoist into the lower cargo hatch and stacked according to the science of stowage. He discovered that Rip had been right, the wood for all its incredible hardness was light of weight. Weak as he still was he could lift and stow a full sized log with no great difficulty. And he thought Weeks was correct in thinking that it would sell on their home world. The color was novel, the durability an asset it would not make fortunes as the Koros stones might, but every bit of profit helped and this cargo might cover their fielding fees on Terra.

Sinbad was in the cargo space when the first of the logs came in. With his usual curiosity the striped tom cat prowled along the wood, sniffing industriously. Suddenly he stopped short, spat and backed away, his spine fur a roughened crest. Having backed as far as the inner door he turned and slunk out. Puzzled, Dane gave the wood a swift inspection. There were no cracks or crevices in the smooth surfaces, but as he stopped over the logs he became conscious of a sharp odor. So this was one scent of the perfumed planet Sinbad did not like. Dane laughed. Maybe they had better have Weeks make a gate of the stuff and slip it across the ramp, keeping Sinbad on ship board. Odd—it wasn't an unpleasant odor—at least to him it wasn't—just sharp and pungent. He sniffed again and was vaguely surprised to discover that it was less noticeable now. Perhaps the wood when taken out of the sunlight lost its scent.

They packed the lower hold solid in accordance with the rules of stowage and locked the hatch before Van Rycke returned from his meeting with the storm priests. When the Cargo-master came back he was followed by two servants bearing between them a chest.

But there was something in Van Rycke's attitude, apparent to those who knew him best, that proclaimed he was not too well pleased with his morning's work. Sparing the feelings of the accompanying storm priests about the offensiveness of the spacer Captain Jellico and Steen Wilcox went out to receive them in the open. Dane watched from the hatch, aware that in his present pariah-hood it would not be wise to venture closer.

The Terran Traders were protesting some course of action that the Salariki were firmly insistent upon. In the end the natives won and Kosti was summoned to carry on board the chest which the servants had brought. Having seen it carried safely inside the spacer, the aliens departed, but Van Rycke was frowning and Jellico's fingers were beating a tattoo on his belt as they came up the ramp.

"I don't like it," Jellico stated as he entered.

"It was none of my doing," Van Rycke snapped. "I'll take risks if I have to—but there's something about this one—" he broke off, two deep lines showing between his thick brows. "Well, you can't teach a sasseral to spit," he ended philosophically. "We'll have to do the best we can."

But Jellico did not look at all happy as he climbed to the control section. And before the hour was out the reason for the Captain's uneasiness was common property throughout the ship.

Having sampled the delights of off-world herbs, the Salariki were determined to not be cut off from their source of supply. Six Terran months from the present Sargolian date would come the great yearly feast of the Fifty Storms, and the priests were agreed that this year their influence and power would be doubled if they could offer the devote certain privileges in the form of Terran plants. Consequently they had produced and forced upon the reluctant Van Rycke the Koros collection of their order, with instructions that it be sold on Terra and the price returned to them in the precious seeds and plants. In vain the Cargo-master and Captain had pointed out that Galactic trade was a chancy thing at the best, that accident might prevent the return of the Queen to Sargol. But the priests had remained adamant and saw in all such arguments only a devious attempt to raise prices. They quoted in their turn the information they had levered out of the Company men—that Traders had their code and that once pay had been given in advance the contract *must* be fulfilled. They, and they alone, wanted the full cargo of the Queen on her next voyage, and they were taking the one way they were sure of achieving that result.

So a fortune in Koros stones which as yet did not rightfully belong to the Traders was now in the Queen's strong-room and her crew were pledged by the strongest possible tie known in their Service to set down on Sargol once more before the allotted time had passed. The Free Traders did not like it, there was even a vaguely superstitious feeling that such a bargain would inevitably draw ill luck to them. But they were left with no choice if they wanted to retain their influence with the Salariki.

"Cutting orbit pretty fine, aren't we?" Ali asked Rip across the mess table. "I saw your two star man sweating it out before he came down to shoot the breeze with us rocket monkeys—"

Rip nodded. "Steen's double checked every computation and some he's done four times." He ran his hands over his close cropped head with a weary gesture. As a semi-invalid he had been herded down with his fellows to swallow the builder Mura had concocted and Tau insisted that they take, but he had been doing half a night's work on the plotter under his chief's exacting eye before he came. "The latest news is that, barring accident, we can make it with about three weeks' grace, give or take a day or two—"

"Barring accident—" the words rang in the air. Here on the frontiers of the star lanes there were so many accidents, so many delays which could put a ship behind schedule. Only on the main star trails did the huge liners or Company ships attempt to keep on regularly timed trips. A Free Trader did not really dare to have an inelastic contract.

"What does Stotz say?" Dane asked Ali.

"He says he can deliver. We don't have the headache about setting a course—you point the nose and we only give her the boost to send her along."

Rip sighed. "Yes—point her nose." He inspected his nails. "Goodbye," he added gravely. "These won't be here by the time we planet here again. I'll have my fingers gnawed off to the first knuckle. Well, we lift at six hours. Pleasant strap down." He drank the last of the stuff in his mug, made a face at the flavor, and got to his feet, due back at his post in control.

Dane, free of duty until the ship earthed, drifted back to his own cabin, sure of part of a night's undisturbed rest before they blasted off. Sinbad was curled on his bunk. For some reason the cat had not been prowling the ship before take-off as he usually did. First he had sat on Van's desk and now he was here, almost as if he wanted human company. Dane picked him up and Sinbad rumbled a purr, arching his head so that it rubbed against the young man's chin in an extremely uncharacteristic show of affection. Smoothing the fur along the cat's jaw line Dane carried him back to the Cargo-master's cabin.

With some hesitation he knocked at the panel and did not step in until he had Van Rycke's muffled invitation. The Cargo-master was stretched on the bunk, two of the take off straps already fastened across his bulk as if he intended to sleep through the blast-off.

"Sinbad, sir. Shall I stow him?"

Van Rycke grunted an assent and Dane dropped the cat in the small hammock which was his particular station, fastening the safety cords. For once Sinbad made no protest but rolled into a ball and was promptly fast asleep. For a moment or two Dane thought about this unnatural behavior and wondered if he should call it to the Cargo-master's attention. Perhaps on Sargol Sinbad had had *his* equivalent of a friendship cup and needed a check-up by Tau.

"Stowage correct?" the question, coming from Van Rycke, was also unusual. The seal would not have been put across the hold lock had its contents not been checked and re-checked.

"Yes, sir," Dane replied woodenly, knowing he was still in the outer darkness. "There was just the wood—we stowed it according to chart."

Van Rycke grunted once more. "Feeling top layer again?"

"Yes, sir. Any orders, sir?"

"No. Blast-off's at six."

"Yes, sir." Dane left the cabin, closing the panel carefully behind him. Would he—or could he—he thought drearily, get back in Van Rycke's profit column again? Sargol had been unlucky as far as he was concerned. First he had made that stupid mistake and then he got sick and now— And now—what *was* the matter? Was it just the general attack of nerves over their voyage and the commitments which forced their haste, or was it something else? He could not rid himself of a vague sense that the Queen was about to take off into real trouble. And he did not like the sensation at all!

chapter 8

HEADACHES

They lifted from Sargol on schedule and went into Hyper also on schedule. From that point on there was nothing to do but wait out the usual dull time of flight between systems and hope that Steen Wilcox had plotted a course which would cut that flight time to a minimum. But this voyage there was little relaxation once they were in Hyper. No matter when Dane dropped into the mess cabin, which was the common meeting place of the spacer, he was apt to find others there before him, usually with a mug of one of Mura's special brews close at hand, speculating about their landing date.

Dane, himself, once he had thrown off the lingering effects of his Sargolian illness, applied time to his studies. When he had first joined the Queen as a recruit straight out of the training Pool, he had speedily learned that all the ten years of intensive study then behind him had only been an introduction to the amount he still had to absorb before he could take his place as an equal with such a trader as Van Rycke—if he had the stuff which would raise him in time to that exalted level. While he had still had his superior's favor he had dared to treat him as an instructor, going to him with perplexing problems of stowage or barter. But now he had no desire to intrude upon the Cargo-master, and doggedly wrestled with the microtapes of old records on his own, painfully working out the why and wherefor for any departure from the regular procedure. He had no inkling of his own future status—whether the return to Terra would find him permanently earthed. And he would ask no questions.

They had been four days of ship's time in Hyper when Dane walked into the mess cabin, tired after his work with old records, to discover no Mura busy in the galley beyond, no brew steaming on the heat coil. Rip sat at the table, his long legs stuck out, his usually happy face very sober.

"What's wrong?" Dane reached for a mug, then seeing no pot of drink, put it back in place.

"Frank's sick—"

"What!" Dane turned. Illness such as they had run into on Sargol had a logical base. But illness on board ship was something else.

"Tau has him isolated. He has a bad headache and he blacked out when he tried to sit up. Tau's running tests."

Dane sat down. "Could be something he ate—"

Rip shook his head. "He wasn't at the feast—remember? And he didn't eat anything from outside, he swore that to Tau. In fact he didn't go dirt much while we were down—"

That was only too true as Dane could now recall. And the fact that the steward had not been at the feast, had not sampled native food products, wiped out the simplest and most comforting reasons for his present collapse.

"What's this about Frank?" Ali stood in the doorway. "He said yesterday that he had a headache. But now Tau has him shut off—"

"He blacked out. Tau's running tests," Rip repeated.

"But he wasn't at that feast." Ali stopped short as the implications of that struck him. "How's Tang feeling?"

"Fine—why?" The Com-tech had come up behind Kamil and was answering for himself. "Why this interest in the state of my health?"

"Frank's down with something—in isolation," Rip replied bluntly. "Did he do anything out of the ordinary when we were off ship?"

For a long moment the other stared at Shannon and then he shook his head. "No. And he wasn't dirt-side to any extent either. So Tau's running tests—" He lapsed into silence. None of them wished to put their thoughts into words.

Dane picked up the microtape he had brought with him and went on down the corridor to return it. The panel of the cargo office was ajar and to his relief he found Van Rycke out. He shoved the tape back in its case and pulled out the next one. Sinbad was there, not in his own private hammock, but sprawled out on the Cargo-master's bunk. He watched Dane lazily, mouthing a silent mew of welcome. For some reason since they had blasted from Sargol the cat had been lazy—as if his adventures afield there had sapped much of his vitality.

"Why aren't you out working?" Dane asked as he leaned over to scratch under a furry chin raised for the benefit of such a caress. "You inspected the hold lately, boy?"

Sinbad merely blinked and after the manner of his species looked infinitely bored. As Dane turned to go the Cargo-master came in. He showed no surprise at Dane's presence. Instead he reached out and fingered the label of the tape Dane had just chosen. After a glance at the identifying symbol he took it out of his assistant's hand, plopped it back in its case, and stood for a moment eyeing the selection of past voyage records. With a tongue-click of satisfaction he pulled out another and tossed it across the desk to Dane.

"See what you can make out of this tangle," he ordered. But Dane's shoulders went back as if some weight had been lifted from them. The old easiness was still lacking, but he was no longer exiled to the outer darkness of Van Rycke's displeasure.

Holding the microtape as if it were a first grade Koros stone Dane went back to his own cabin, snapped the tape into his reader, adjusted the ear buttons and lay back on his bunk to listen.

He was deep in the intricacy of a deal so complicated that he was lost after the first two moves, when he opened his eyes to see Ali at the door panel. The Engineer-apprentice made an emphatic beckoning wave and Dane slipped off the ear buttons.

"What is it?" His question lacked a cordial note.

"I've got to have help." Ali was terse. "Kosti's blacked out!"

"What!" Dane sat up and dropped his feet to the deck in almost one movement.

"I can't shift him alone," Ali stated the obvious. The giant jetman was almost double his size. "We must get him to his quarters. And I won't ask Stotz—"

For a perfectly good reason Dane knew. An assistant—two of the apprentices—could go sick, but their officers continued good health meant the most to the Queen. If some infection were aboard it would be better for Ali and himself to be exposed, than to have Johan Stotz with all his encyclopedic knowledge of the ship's engines contract any disease.

They found the jetman half sitting, half lying in the short foot or so of corridor which led to his own cubby. He had been making for his quarters when the seizure had taken him. And by the time the two reached his side, he was beginning to come around, moaning, his hands going to his head.

Together they got him on his feet and guided him to his bunk where he collapsed again, a dead weight they had to push into place. Dane looked at Ali—

"Tau?"

"Haven't had time to call him yet." Ali was jerking at the thigh straps which fastened Kosti's space boots.

"I'll go." Glad for the task Dane sped up the ladder to the next section and threaded the narrow side hall to the Medic's cabin where he knocked on the panel.

There was a pause before Craig Tau looked out, deep lines of weariness bracketing his mouth, etched between his eyes.

"Kosti, sir," Dane gave his bad news quickly. "He's collapsed. We got him to his cabin—"

Tau showed no sign of surprise. His hand shot out for his kit. "You touched him?" At the other's nod he added an order. "Stay in your quarters until I have a chance to look you over—understand?"

Dane had no chance to answer, the Medic was already on his way. He went to his own cabin, understanding the reason for his imprisonment, but inwardly rebelling against it. Rather than sit idle he snapped on the reader—but, although facts and figures were dunned into his ears—he really heard very little. He couldn't apply himself—not with a new specter leering at him from the bulkhead.

The dangers of the space lanes were not to be numbered, death walked among the stars a familiar companion of all spacemen. And to the Free Trader it was the extra and invisible crewman on every ship that raised. But there were deaths and deaths— And Dane could not forget the gruesome legends Van Rycke collected avidly as his hobby—had recorded in his private library of the folk lore of space.

Stories such as that of the ghostly "New Hope" carrying refugees from the first Martian Rebellion—the ship which had lifted for the stars but had never arrived, which wandered for a timeless eternity, a derelict in free fall, its ports closed but the warning "dead" lights on at its nose—a ship which through five centuries had been sighted only by a spacer in similar distress. Such stories were numerous. There were other tales of "plague" ships wandering free with their dead crews, or discovered and shot into some sun by a Patrol cruiser so that they might not carry their infection farther. Plague—the nebulous "worst" the Traders had to face. Dane screwed his eyes shut, tried to concentrate upon the droning voice in his ears, but he could not control his thoughts nor—his fears.

At a touch on his arm he started so wildly that he jerked the cord loose from the reader and sat up, somewhat shamefaced, to greet Tau. At the Medic's orders he stripped for one of the most complete examinations he had ever undergone outside a quarantine port. It included an almost microscopic inspection of the skin on his neck and shoulders, but when Tau had done he gave a sigh of relief.

"Well, you haven't got it—at least you don't show any signs yet," he amended his first statement almost before the words were out of his mouth.

"What were you looking for?"

Tau took time out to explain. "Here," his fingers touched the small hollow at the base of Dane's throat and then swung him around and indicated two places on the back of his neck and under his shoulder blades. "Kosti and Mura both have red eruptions here. It's as if they have been given an injection of some narcotic." Tau sat down on the jump seat while Dane dressed. "Kosti was dirt-side—he might have picked up something—"

"But Mura—"

"That's it!" Tau brought his fist down on the edge of the bunk. "Frank hardly left the ship—yet he showed the first signs. On the other hand you are all right so far and you were off ship. And Ali's clean and he was with you on the hunt. We'll just have to wait and see." He got up wearily. "If your head begins to ache," he told Dane, "you get back here in a hurry and stay put—understand?"

As Dane learned all the other members of the crew were given the same type of inspection. But none of them showed the characteristic marks which meant trouble. They were on course for Terra—but—and that but must have loomed large in all their minds—once there would they be allowed to land? Could they even hope for a hearing? Plague ship—Tau must find the answer before they came into normal space about their own solar system or they were in for such trouble as made a broken contract seem the simplest of mishaps.

Kosti and Mura were in isolation. There were volunteers for nursing and Tau, unable to be in two places at once, finally picked Weeks to look after his crewmate in the engineering section.

There was doubling up of duties. Tau could no longer share with Mura the care of the hydro garden so Van Rycke took over. While Dane found himself in charge of the galley and, while he did not have Mura's deft hand at disguising the monotonous concentrates to the point they resembled fresh food, after a day or two he began to experiment cautiously and produced a stew which brought some short words of appreciation from Captain Jellico.

They all breathed a sigh of relief when, after three days, no more signs of the mysterious illness showed on new members of the crew. It became routine to parade before Tau stripped to the waist each morning for the inspection of the danger points, and the Medic's vigilance did not relax.

In the meantime neither Mura nor Kosti appeared to suffer. Once the initial stages of headaches and blackouts were passed, the patients lapsed into a semi-conscious state as if they were under sedation of some type. They would eat, if the food was placed in their mouths, but they did not seem to know what was going on about them, nor did they answer when spoken to.

Tau, between visits to them, worked feverishly in his tiny lab, analyzing blood samples, reading the records of obscure diseases, trying to find the reason for their attacks. But as yet his discoveries were exactly nothing. He had come out of his quarters and sat in limp exhaustion at the mess table while Dane placed before him a mug of stimulating caf-hag.

"I don't get it!" The Medic addressed the table top rather than the amateur cook. "It's a poison of some kind. Kosti went dirt-side—Mura didn't. Yet Mura came down with it first. And we didn't ship any food from Sargol. Neither did he eat any while we were there. Unless he did and we didn't know about it. If I could just bring him to long enough to answer a couple of questions!" Sighing he dropped his weary head on his folded arms and within seconds was asleep.

Dane put the mug back on the heating unit and sat down at the other end of the table. He did not have the heart to shake Tau into wakefulness—let the poor devil get a slice of bunk time, he certainly needed it after the fatigues of the past four days.

Van Rycke passed along the corridor on his way to the hydro,

Sinbad at his heels. But in a moment the cat was back, leaping up on Dane's knee. He did not curl up, but rubbed against the young man's arm, finally reaching up with a paw to touch Dane's chin, uttering one of the soundless mews which were his bid for attention.

"What's the matter, boy?" Dane fondled the cat's ears. "You haven't got a headache—have you?" In that second a wild surmise came into his mind. Sinbad had been planet-side on Sargol as much as he could, and on ship board he was equally at home in all their cabins—could he be the carrier of the disease?

A good idea—only if it were true, then logically the second victim should have been Van, or Dane—where as Sinbad lingered most of the time in their cabins—not Kosti. The cat, as far as he knew, had never shown any particular fondness for the jetman and certainly did not sleep in Karl's quarters. No—that point did not fit. But he would mention it to Tau—no use overlooking anything—no matter how wild.

It was the sequence of victims which puzzled them all. As far as Tau had been able to discover Mura and Kosti had nothing much in common except that they were crewmates on the same spacer. They did not bunk in the same section, their fields of labor were totally different, they had no special food or drink tastes in common, they were not even of the same race. Frank Mura was one of the few descendants of a mysterious (or now mysterious) people who had had their home on a series of islands in one of Terra's seas, islands which almost a hundred years before had been swallowed up in a series of world-rending quakes—Japan was the ancient name of that nation. While Karl Kosti had come from the once thickly populated land masses half the planet away which had borne the geographical name of "Europe." No, all the way along the two victims had only very general meeting points—they both shipped on the Solar Queen and they were both of Terran birth.

Tau stirred and sat up, blinking bemusedly at Dane, then pushed back his wiry black hair and assumed a measure of alertness. Dane dropped the now purring cat in the Medic's lap and in a few sentences outlined his suspicion. Tau's hands closed about Sinbad.

"There's a chance in that—" He looked a little less beat and he drank thirstily from the mug Dave gave him for the second time. Then he hurried out with Sinbad under one arm—bound for his lab.

Dane slicked up the galley, trying to put things away as neatly as Mura kept them. He didn't have much faith in the Sinbad lead, but in this case everything must be checked out.

When the Medic did not appear during the rest of the ship's day Dane was not greatly concerned. But he was alerted to trouble when Ali came in with an inquiry and a complaint.

"Seen anything of Craig?"

"He's in the lab," Dane answered.

"He didn't answer my knock," Ali protested. "And Weeks says he hasn't been in to see Karl all day—"

That did catch Dane's attention. Had his half hunch been right? Was Tau on the trail of a discovery which had kept him chained to the lab? But it wasn't like the Medic not to look in on his patients.

"You're sure he isn't in the lab?"

"I told you that he didn't answer my knock. I didn't open the panel—" But now Ali was already in the corridor heading back the way he had come, with Dane on his heels, an unwelcome explanation for that silence in both their minds. And their fears were reinforced by what they heard as they approached the panel—a low moan wrung out of unbearable pain. Dane thrust the sliding door open.

Tau had slipped from his stool to the floor. His hands were at his head which rolled from side to side as if he were trying to quiet some agony. Dane stripped down the Medic's under tunic. There was no need to make a careful examination, in the hollow of Craig Tau's throat was the tell-tale red blotch.

"Sinbad!" Dane glance about the cabin. "Did Sinbad get out past you?" he demanded of the puzzled Ali.

"No—I haven't seen him all day—"

Yet the cat was nowhere in the tiny cabin and it had no concealed hiding place. To make doubly sure Dane secured the panel before they carried Tau to his bunk. The Medic had blacked out again, passed into the lethargic second stage of the malady. At least he was out of the pain which appeared to be the worst symptom of the disease.

"It must be Sinbad!" Dane said as he made his report directly to Captain Jellico. "And yet—"

"Yes, he's been staying in Van's cabin," the Captain mused. "And you've handled him, he slept on your bunk. Yet you and Van are all right. I don't understand that. Anyway—to be on the safe side—we'd better find and isolate him before—"

He didn't have to underline any words for the grim-faced men who listened. With Tau—their one hope of fighting the disease gone—they had a black future facing them.

They did not have to search for Sinbad. Dane coming down to his own section found the cat crouched before the panel of Van Rycke's cabin, his eyes glued to the thin crack of the door. Dane scooped him up and took him to the small cargo space intended for the safeguarding of choice items of commerce. To his vast surprise Sinbad began fighting wildly as he opened the hatch, kicking and then slashing with ready claws. The cat seemed to go mad and Dane had all he could do to shut him in. When he snapped the panel he heard Sinbad launch himself against the barrier as if to batter his way out. Dane, blood welling in several deep scratches, went in search of first aid. But some suspicion led him to pause as he passed Van Rycke's door. And when his knock brought no answer he pushed the panel open.

Van Rycke lay on his bunk, his eyes half closed in a way which had become only too familiar to the crew of the Solar Queen. And Dane knew that when he looked for it he would find the mark of the strange plague on the Cargo-master's body.

chapter 9

PLAGUE!

Jellico and Steen Wilcox poured over the few notes Tau had made before he was stricken. But apparently the Medic had found nothing to indicate that Sinbad was the carrier of any disease. Meanwhile the Captain gave orders for the cat to be confined. A difficult task—since Sinbad crouched close to the door of the storage cabin and was ready to dart out when food was taken in for him. Once he got a good way down the corridor before Dane was able to corner and return him to keeping.

Dane, Ali and Weeks took on the full care of the four sick men, leaving the few regular duties of the ship to the senior officers, while Rip was installed in charge of the hydro garden.

Mura, the first to be taken ill, showed no change. He was semi-conscious, he swallowed food if it were put in his mouth, he responded to nothing around him. And Kosti, Tau, and Van Rycke followed the same pattern. They still held morning inspection of those on their feet for signs of a new outbreak, but when no one else went down during the next two days, they regained a faint spark of hope.

Hope which was snapped out when Ali brought the news that Stotz could not be roused and must have taken ill during a sleep period. One more inert patient was added to the list—and nothing learned about how he was infected. Except that they could eliminate Sinbad, since the cat had been in custody during the time Stotz had apparently contracted the disease.

Weeks, Ali and Dane, though they were in constant contact with the sick men, and though Dane had repeatedly handled Sinbad, continued to be immune. A fact, Dane thought more than once, which must have significance—if someone with Tau's medical knowledge had been able to study it. By all rights they should be the most susceptible—but the opposite seemed true. And Wilcox duly noted that fact among the data they had recorded.

It became a matter of watching each other, waiting for another collapse. And they were not surprised when Tang Ya reeled into the mess, his face livid and drawn with pain. Rip and Dane got him to his cabin before he blacked out. But all they could learn from him during the interval before he lost consciousness was that his head was bursting and he couldn't stand it. Over his limp body they stared at one another bleakly.

"Six down," Ali observed, "and six to go. How do you feel?"

"Tired, that's all. What I don't understand is that once they go into this stupor they just stay. They don't get any worse, they have no rise in temperature—it's as if they are in a modified form of cold sleep!"

"How is Tang?" Rip asked from the corridor.

"Usual pattern," Ali answered. "He's sleeping. Got a pain, Fella?"

Rip shook his head. "Right as a Com-unit. I don't get it. Why does it strike Tang who didn't even hit dirt much—and yet you keep on—?"

Dane grimmaced. "If we had an answer to that, maybe we'd know what caused the whole thing—"

Ali's eyes narrowed. He was staring straight at the unconscious Com-tech as if he did not see that supine body at all.
"I wonder if we've been salted—" he said slowly.

"We've been *what?*" Dane demanded.

"Look here, we three—with Weeks—drank that brew of the
Salariki, didn't we? And we—"

"Were as sick as Venusian gobblers afterwards," agreed Rip.
Light dawned. "Do you mean—" began Dane.

"So that's it!" flashed Rip.

"It might just be," Ali said. "Do you remember how the
settlers on Camblyne brought their Terran cattle through
the first year? They fed them salt mixed with fansel grass. The
result was that the herds didn't take the fansel grass fever
when they turned them out to pasture in the dry season. All
right, maybe we had our 'salt' in that drink. The fansel-salt
makes the cattle filthy sick when it's forced down their throats,
but after they recover they're immune to the fever. And nobody
on Camblyne buys unsalted cattle now."

"It sounds logical," admitted Rip. "But how are we going
to prove it?"

Ali's face was black once more. "Probably by elimination,"
he said morosely. "If we keep our feet and all the rest go down
—that's our proof."

"But we ought to be able to do something—" protested
Shannon.

"Just how?" Ali's slender brows arched. "Do you have a
gallon of that Salariki brew on board you can serve out? We
don't know what was in it. Nor are we sure that this whole
idea has any value."

All of them had had first aid and basic preventive medicine
as part of their training, but the more advanced laboratory ex-
perimentation was beyond their knowledge and skill. Had
Tau still been on his feet perhaps he could have traced that
lead and brought order out of the chaos which was closing
in upon the Solar Queen. But, though they reported their suggestion to the Captain, Jellico was powerless to do anything
about it. If the four who had shared that upsetting friendship

cup were immune to the doom which now overhung the ship, there was no possible way for them to discover why or how.

Ship's time came to have little meaning. And they were not surprised when Steen Wilcox slipped from his seat before the computer—to be stowed away with what had become a familiar procedure. Only Jellico withstood the contagion apart from the younger four, taking his turn at caring for the helpless men. There was no change in their condition. They neither roused nor grew worse as the hours and then the days sped by. But each of those units of time in passing brought them nearer to greater danger. Sooner or later they must make the transition out of Hyper into system space, and the jump out of warp was something not even a veteran took lightly. Rip's round face thinned while they watched. Jellico was still functioning. But if the Captain collapsed the whole responsibility for the snap-out would fall directly on Shannon. An infinitesimal error would condemn them to almost hopeless wandering—perhaps for ever.

Dane and Ali relieved Rip of all duty but that which kept him chained in Wilcox's chair before the computers. He went over and over the data of the course the Astrogator had set. And Captain Jellico, his eyes sunk in dark pits, checked and rechecked.

When the fatal moment came Ali manned the engine room with Weeks at his elbow to tend the controls the acting-Engineer could not reach. And Dane, having seen the sick all safely stowed in crash webbing, came up to the control cabin, riding out the transfer in Tang Ya's place.

Rip's voice hoarsened into a croak, calling out the data. Dane, though he had had basic theory, was completely lost before Shannon had finished the first set of co-ordinates. But Jellico replied, hands playing across the pilot's board.

"Stand-by for snap-out—" the croak went down to the engines where Ali now held Stotz's post.

"Engines ready!" The voice came back, thinned by its journey from the Queen's interior.

"Ought-five-nine—" That was Jellico.

Dane found himself suddenly unable to watch. He shut his eyes and braced himself against the vertigo of snap-out. It came and he whirled sickeningly through unstable space. Then he was sitting in the laced Com-tech's seat looking at Rip.

Runnels of sweat streaked Shannon's brown face. There was a damp patch darkening his tunic between his shoulder blades, a patch which it would take both of Dane's hands to cover.

For a moment he did not raise his head to look at the vision plate which would tell them whether or not they had made it. But when he did familiar constellations made the patterns they knew. They were out—and they couldn't be too far off the course Wilcox had plotted. There was still the system run to make—but snap-out was behind them. Rip gave a deep sigh and buried his head in his hands.

With a throb of fear Dane unhooked his safety belt and hurried over to him. When he clutched at Shannon's shoulder the Astrogator-apprentice's head rolled limply. Was Rip down with the illness too? But the other muttered and opened his eyes.

"Does your head ache?" Dane shook him.

"Head? No—" Rip's words came drowsily. "Jus' sleepy—so sleepy—"

He did not seem to be in pain. But Dane's hands were shaking as he hoisted the other out of his seat and half carried-half led him to his cabin, praying as he went that it was only fatigue and not the disease. The ship was on auto now until Jellico as pilot set a course—

Dane got Rip down on the bunk and stripped off his tunic. The fine-drawn face of the sleeper looked wan against the foam rest, and he snuggled into the softness like a child as he turned over and curled up. But his skin was clear—it was real sleep and not the plague which had claimed him.

Impulse sent Dane back to the control cabin. He was not an experienced pilot officer, but there might be some assistance he could offer the Captain now that Rip was washed out, perhaps for hours.

Jellico hunched before the smaller computer, feeding pilot

tape into its slot. His face was a skull under a thin coating of skin, the bones marking it sharply at jaw, nose and eye socket.

"Shannon down?" His voice was a mere whisper of its powerful self, he did not turn his head.

"He's just worn out, sir," Dane hastened to give reassurance. "The marks aren't on him."

"When he comes around tell him the co-ords are in," Jellico murmured. "See he checks course in ten hours—"

"But, sir—" Dane's protest failed as he watched the Captain struggle to his feet, pulling himself up with shaking hands. As Thorson reached forward to steady the other, one of those hands tore at tunic collar, ripping loose the sealing—

There was no need for explanation—the red splotch signaled from Jellico's sweating throat. He kept his feet, holding out against the waves of pain by sheer will power. Then Dane had a grip on him, got him away from the computer, hoping he could keep him going until they reached Jellico's cabin.

Somehow they made that journey, being greeted with raucous screams from the Hoobat. Furiously Dane slapped the cage, setting it to swinging and so silencing the creature which stared at him with round, malignant eyes as he got the Captain to bed.

Only four of them on their feet now, Dane thought bleakly as he left the cabin. If Rip came out of it in time they could land—Dane's breath caught as he made himself face up to the fact that Shannon might be ill, that it might be up to *him* to bring the Queen in for a landing. And in where? The Terra quarantine was Luna City on the Moon. But let them signal for a set-down there—let them describe what had happened and they might face death as a plague ship.

Wearily he climbed down to the mess cabin to discover Weeks and Ali there before him. They did not look up as he entered.

"Old Man's got it," he reported.

"Rip?" was Ali's crossing question.

"Asleep. He passed out—"

"What!" Weeks swung around.

"Worn out," Dane amended. "Captain fed in a pilot tape before he gave up."

"So—now we are three," was Ali's comment. "Where do we set down—Luna City?"

"If they let us," Dane hinted at the worst.

"But they've got to let us!" Weeks exclaimed. "We can't just wander around out here—"

"It's been done," Ali reminded them brutally and that silenced Weeks.

"Did the Old Man set Luna?" After a long pause Ali inquired.

"I didn't check," Dane confessed. "He was giving out and I had to get him to his bunk."

"It might be well to know." The Engineer-apprentice got up, his movements lacking much of the elastic spring which was normally his. When he climbed to control both the others followed him.

Ali's slender fingers played across a set of keys and in the small screen mounting on the computer a set of figures appeared. Dane took up the master course book, read the connotation and blinked.

"Not Luna?" Ali asked.

"No. But I don't understand. This must be for somewhere in the asteroid belt."

Ali's lips stretched into a pale caricature of a smile. "Good for the Old Man, he still had his wits about him, even after the bug bit him!"

"But why are we going to the asteroids?" Weeks asked reasonably enough. "There're Medics at Luna City—they can help us—"

"They can handle known diseases," Ali pointed out. "But what of the Code?"

Weeks dropped into the Com-tech's place as if some of the stiffening had vanished from his thin but sturdy legs. "They wouldn't do that—" he protested, but his eyes said that he knew that they might—they well might.

"Oh, no? Face the facts, man," Ali sounded almost savage. "We come from a frontier planet, we're a plague ship—"

He did not have to underline that. They all knew too well the danger in which they now stood.

"Nobody's died yet," Weeks tried to find an opening in the net being drawn about them.

"And nobody's recovered," Ali crushed that thread of hope. "We don't know what it is, how it is contracted—anything about it. Let us make a report saying that and you know what will happen—don't you?"

They weren't sure of the details, but they could guess.

"So I say," Ali continued, "the Old Man was right when he set us on an evasion course. If we can stay out until we really know what is the matter we'll have some chance of talking over the high brass at Luna when we do planet—"

In the end they decided not to interfere with the course the Captain had set. It would take them into the fringes of solar civilization, but give them a fighting chance at solving their problem before they had to report to the authorities. In the meantime they tended their charges, let Rip sleep, and watched each other with desperate but hidden intentness, ready for another to be stricken. However they remained, although almost stupid with fatigue at times, reasonably healthy. Time was proving that their guess had been correct—they had been somehow inoculated against the germ or virus which had struck the ship.

Rip slept for twenty-four hours, ship time, and then came into the mess cabin ravenously hungry, to catch up on both food and news. And he refused to join with the prevailing pessimistic view of the future. Instead he was sure that their own immunity having been proven, they had a talking point to use with the medical officials at Luna and he was eager to alter course directly for the quarantine station. Only the combined arguments of the other three made him, unwillingly, agree to a short delay.

And how grateful they should be for Captain Jellico's foresight they learned within the next day. Ali was at the com-unit, trying to pick up Solarian news reports. When the red alert flashed on throughout the ship it brought the others hurrying to the control cabin. The code squeaks were magnified as Ali switched on the receiver full strength, to be translated as he pressed a second button.

"Repeat, repeat, repeat. Free Trader, Solar Queen, Terra Registry 65-724910-Jk, suspected plague ship—took off from infected planet. Warn off—warn off—report such ship to Luna Station. Solar Queen from infected planet—to be warned off and reported." The same message was repeated three times before going off ether.

The four in the control cabin looked at each other blankly.

"But," Dane broke the silence, "how did they know? We haven't reported in—"

"The Eysies!" Ali had the answer ready. "That I-S ship must be having the same sort of trouble and reported to her Company. They would include us in their report and believe that we were infected too—or it would be easy to convince the authorities that we were."

"I wonder," Rip's eyes were narrowed slits as he leaned back against the wall. "Look at the facts. The Survey ship which charted Sargol—they were dirt-side there about three—four months. Yet they gave it a clean bill of health and put it up for trading rights auction. Then Cam bought those rights—he made at least two trips in and out before he was blasted on Limbo. No infection bothered him or Survey—"

"But you've got to admit it hit us," Weeks protested.

"Yes, and the Eysie ship was able to foresee it—report us before we snapped out of Hyper. Sounds almost as if they expected us to carry plague, doesn't it?" Shannon wanted to know.

"Planted?" Ali frowned at the banks of controls. "But how —no Eysie came on board—no Salarik either, except for the cub who showed us what they thought of catnip."

Rip shrugged. "How would I know how they did—" he was beginning when Dane cut in:

"If they didn't know about our immunity the *Queen* might

stay in Hyper and never come out—there wouldn't be anyone to set the snap-out."

"Right enough. But on the chance that somebody did keep on his feet and bring her home, they were ready with a cover. If no one raises a howl Sargol will be written off the charts as infected. I-S sits on her tail fins a year or so and then she promotes an investigation before the Board. The Survey records are trotted out—no infection recorded. So they send in a Patrol Probe. Everything is all right—so it wasn't the planet after all —it was that dirty old Free Trader. And she's out of the way. I-S gets the Koros trade all square and legal and we're no longer around to worry about! Neat as a Salariki net cast—and right around our collective throats, my friends!"

"So what do we do now?" Weeks wanted to know.

"We keep on the Old Man's course, get lost in the asteroids until we can do some heavy thinking and see a way out. But if I-S gave us this prize package, some trace of its origin is still aboard. And if we can find that—why, then we have something to start from."

"Mura went down first—and then Karl. Nothing in common," the old problem faced Dane for the hundredth time.

"No. But," Ali arose from his place at the com-unit. "I'd suggest a real search of first Frank's and then Karl's quarters. A regular turn out down to the bare walls of their cabins. Are you with me?"

"Fly boy, we're ahead of you!" Rip contributed, already at the door panel. "Down to the bare walls it is."

chapter 10

E-STAT LANDING

Since Mura was in the isolation of ship sick bay the stripping of his cabin was a relatively simple job. But, though Rip and Dane went over it literally by inches, they found nothing un-usual—in fact nothing from Sargol except a small twig of the red wood which lay on the steward's worktable where he had been fashioning something to incorporate in one of his minia-ture fairy landscapes, to be imprisoned for all time in a plasta-bubble. Dane turned this around in his fingers. Because it was the only link with the perfumed planet he couldn't help but feel that it had some importance.

But Kosti had not shown any interest in the wood. And he, himself, and Weeks had handled it freely *before* they had tasted Groft's friendship cup and had no ill effects—so it couldn't be the wood. Dane put the twig back on the work table and snapped the protecting cover over the delicate tools—never realizing until days later how very close he had been in that moment to the solution of their problem.

After two hours of shifting every one of the steward's belongings, of crawling on hands and knees about the deck and climbing to inspect perfectly bare walls, they had found exactly nothing. Rip sat down on the end of the denuded bunk.

"There's the hydro—Frank spent a lot of time in there—and the storeroom," he told the places off on his fingers. "The galley and the mess cabin."

Those had been the extent of Mura's world. They could search the storeroom, the galley and the mess cabin—but to interfere with the hydro would endanger their air supply. It was for that very reason that they now looked at each other in startled surmise.

"The perfect place to plant something!" Dane spoke first.

Rip's teeth caught his underlip. The hydro—something planted there could not be routed out unless they made a landing on a port field and had the whole section stripped.

"Devilish—" Rip's mobile lips drew tight. "But how could they do it?"

Dane didn't see how it could have been done either. No one but the Queen's own crew had been on board the ship during their entire stay on Sargol, except for the young Salarik. Could that cub have brought something? But he and Mura had been with the youngster every minute that he had been in the hydro. To the best of Dane's memory the cub had touched nothing and had been there only for a few moments. That had been before the feast also—

Rip got to his feet. "We can't strip the hydro in space," he pointed out the obvious quietly.

Dane had the answer. "Then we've got to earth!"

"You heard that warn-off. If we try it—"

"What about an Emergency station?"

Rip stood very still, his big hands locked about the buckle of his arms belt. Then, without another word, he went out of the cabin and at a pounding pace up the ladder, bound for the Captain's cabin and the records Jellico kept there. It was such a slim chance—but it was better than none at all.

Dane shouldered into the small space in his wake, to find

Rip making a selection from the astrogation tapes. There were E-Stats among the asteroids—points prospectors or small traders in sudden difficulties might contact for supplies or repairs. The big Companies maintained their own—the Patrol had several for independents.

"No Patrol one—"

Rip managed a smile. "I haven't gone space whirly yet," was his comment. He was feeding a tape into the reader on the Captain's desk. In the cage over his head the blue Hoobat squatted watching him intently—for the first time since Dane could remember showing no sign of resentment by weird screams or wild spitting.

"Patrol E-Stat A-54—" the reader squeaked. Rip hit a key and the wire clicked to the next entry. "Combine E-Stat—" Another punch and click. "Patrol E-Stat A-55—" punch-click. "Inter-Solar—" this time Rip's hand did not hit the key and the squeak continued—"Co-ordinates—" Rip reached for a steelo and jotted down the list of figures.

"Got to compare this with our present course—"

"But that's an I-S Stat," began Dane and then he laughed as the justice of such a move struck him. They did not dare set the Queen down at any Patrol Station. But a Company one which would be manned by only two or three men and not expecting any but their own people—and I-S owed them help now!

"There may be trouble," he said, not that he would have any regrets if there was. If the Eysies were responsible for the present plight of the Queen he would welcome trouble, the kind which would plant his fists on some sneering Eysie face.

"We'll see about that when we come to it," Rip went on to the control cabin with his figures. Carefully he punched the combination on the plotter and watched it be compared with the course Jellico had set before his collapse.

"Good enough," he commented as the result flashed on. "We can make it without using too much fuel—"

"Make what?" That was Ali up from the search of Kosti's quarters. "Nothing," he gave his report of what he had found there and then returned to the earlier question. "Make what?"

Swiftly Dane outlined their suspicions—that the seat of the trouble lay in the hydro and that they should clean out that section, drawing upon emergency materials at the I-S E-Stat.

"Sounds all right. But you know what they do to pirates?" inquired the Engineer-apprentice.

Space law came into Dane's field, he needed no prompting. "Any ship in emergency," he recited automatically, "may claim supplies from the nearest E-Stat—paying for them when the voyage is completed."

"That means any Patrol E-Stat. The Companies' are private property."

"But," Dane pointed out triumphantly, "the law doesn't say so—there is nothing about any difference between Company and Patrol E-Stat in the law—"

"He's right," Rip agreed. "That law was framed when only the Patrol had such stations. Companies put them in later to save tax—remember? Legally we're all right."

"Unless the agents on duty raise a howl," Ali amended. "Oh, don't give me that look, Rip. I'm not sounding any warn-off on this, but I just want you to be prepared to find a cruiser riding our fins and giving us the hot flash as bandits. If you want to spoil the Eysies, I'm all for it. Got a stat of theirs pinpointed?"

Rip pointed to the figures on the computer. "There she is. We can set down in about five hours' ship time. How long will it take to strip the hydro and re-install?"

"How can I tell?" Ali sounded irritable. "I can give you oxgy for quarters for about two hours. Depends upon how fast we can move. No telling until we make a start."

He started for the corridor and then added over his shoulder: "You'll have to answer a com challenge—thought about that?"

"Why?" Rip asked. "It might be com repairs bringing us in. They won't be expecting trouble and we will—we'll have the advantage."

But Ali was not to be shaken out of his usual dim view of the future. "All right—so we land, blaster in hand, and take the place. And they get off one little squeak to the Patrol. Well, a short life but an interesting one. And we'll make all the Video channels for sure when we go out with rockets blasting. Nothing like having a little excitement to break the dull routine of a voyage."

"We aren't going to, are we—" Dane protested, "land armed, I mean?"

Ali stared at him and Rip, to Dane's surprise, did not immediately repudiate that thought.

"Sleep rods, certainly," the Astrogator-apprentice said after a pause. "We'll have to be prepared for the moment when they find out who we are. And you can't re-set a hydro in a few minutes, not when we have to keep oxgy on for the others. If we were able to turn that off and work in suits it'd be a quicker job—we could dump before we set down and then pile it in at once. But this way it's going to be piece work. And it all depends on the agents at the Stat whether we have trouble or not."

"We had better break out the suits now," Ali added to Rip's estimate of the situation. "If we set down and pile out wearing suits at once it will build up our tale of being poor wrecked spacemen—"

Sleep rods or not, Dane thought to himself, the whole plan was one born of desperation. It would depend upon who manned the E-Stat and how fast the Free Traders could move once the Queen touched her fins to earth.

"Knock out their coms," that was Ali continuing to plan. "Do that first and then we don't have to worry about someone calling in the Patrol."

Rip stretched. For the first time in hours he seemed to have returned to his usual placid self. "Good thing somebody in this spacer watches Video serials—Ali, you can brief us on all the latest tricks of space pirates. Nothing is so wildly improbable that you can't make use of it sometime during a checkered career."

He glanced over the board before he brought his hand down

on a single key set a distance apart from the other controls. "Put some local color into it," was his comment.

Dane understood. Rip had turned on the distress signal at the Queen's nose. When she set down on the Stat field she would be flaming a banner of trouble. Next to the wan dead lights, set only when a ship had no hope of ever reaching port at all, that signal was one every spacer dreaded having to flash. But it was *not* the dead lights—not yet for the Queen.

Working together they brought out the space suits and readied them at the hatch. Then Weeks and Dane took up the task of tending their unconscious charges while Rip and Ali prepared for landing.

There was no change in the sleepers. And in Jellico's cabin even Queex appeared to be influenced by the plight of its master, for instead of greeting Dane with its normal aspect of rage, the Hoobat stayed quiescent on the floor of its cage, its top claws hooked about two of the wires, its protruding eyes staring out into the room with what seemed closed to a malignant intelligence. It did not even spit as Dane passed under its abode to pour thin soup into his patient.

As for Sinbad, the cat had retreated to Dane's cabin and steadily refused to leave the quarters he had chosen, resisting with tooth and claw the one time Dane had tried to take him back to Van Rycke's office and his own hammock there. After-wards the Cargo-apprentice did not try to evict him—there was comfort in seeing that plump gray body curled on the bunk he had little chance to use.

His nursing duties performed for the moment, Dane ventured into the hydro. He was practiced in tending this vital heart of the ship's air supply. But outfitting a hydro was something else again. In his cadet years he had aided in such a program at least twice as a matter of learning the basic training of the Service. But then they had had unlimited supplies to draw on and the action had taken place under no more pressure than that exerted by the instructors. Now it was going to be a far more tricky job—

He went slowly down the aisle between the banks of green

things. Plants from all over the Galaxy, grown for their contribution to the air renewal—as well as side products such as fresh fruit and vegetables, were banked there. The sweet odor of their verdant life was strong. But how could any of the four now on duty tell what was rightfully there and what might have been brought in? And could they be sure anything *had* been introduced?

Dane stood there, his eyes searching those lines of greens—such a mixture of greens from the familiar shade of Terra's fields to greens tinged with shades first bestowed by other suns on other worlds—looking for one which was alien enough to be noticeable. Only Mura, who knew this garden as he knew his own cabin, could have differentiated between them. They would just dump everything and trust to luck—

He was suddenly aware of a slight movement in the banks—a shivering of stem, quiver of leaf. The mere act of his passing had set some sensitive plant to register his presence. A lacy, fern-like thing was contracting its fronds into balls. He should not stay—disturbing the peace of the hydro. But it made little difference now—within a matter of hours all this luxuriance would be thrust out to die and they would have to depend upon canned oxgy and algae tanks. Too bad—the hydro represented much time and labor on Mura's part and Tau had medical plants growing there he had been observing for a long time.

As Dane closed the door behind him, seeing the line of balled fern which had marked his passage, he heard a faint rustling, a sound as if a wind had swept across the green room within. That imagination which was a Trader's asset (when it was kept within bounds) suggested that the plants inside guessed— With a frown for his own sentimentality, Dane strode down the corridor and climbed to check with Rip in control.

The Astrogator-apprentice had his own problems. To bring the Queen down on the circumscribed field of an E-Stat—without a guide beam to ride in—since if they contacted the Stat they must reveal their *own* com was working and they would have to answer questions—was the sort of test even a seasoned pilot would tense over. Yet Rip was sitting now in the Captain's place, his broad hands spread out on the edge of the control board waiting. And below in the engine room Ali was in Stotz's place ready to fire and cut rockets at order. Of course they were both several years ahead of him in Service, Dane knew. But he wondered at their quick assumption of responsibility and whether he himself could ever reach that point of self-confidence—his memory turning to the bad mistake he had made on Sargol.

There was the sharp note of a warning gong, the flash of red light on the control board. They were off automatic, from here on in it was all Rip's work. Dane strapped down at the silent com-unit and was startled a moment later when it spat words at him, translated from space code.

"Identify—identify— I-S E-Stat calling spacer—identify—"

So compelling was that demand that Dane's fingers went to the answer key before he remembered and snatched them back, to fold his hands in his lap.

"Identify—" the expressionless voice of the translator droned over their heads.

Rip's hands were on the control board, playing the buttons there with the precision of a musician creating some symphonic masterpiece. And the Queen was alive, now quivering through her stout plates, coming into a landing.

Dane watched the visa plate. The E-Stat asteroid was of a reasonable size, but in their eyes it was a bleak, torn mote of stuff swimming through vast emptiness.

"Identify—" the drone heightened in pitch.

Rip's lips were compressed, he made quick calculations. And Dane saw that, though Jellico was the master, Rip was fully fit to follow in the Captain's boot prints.

There was a sudden silence in the cabin—the demand had stopped. The agents below must now have realized that the ship with the distress signals blazing on her nose was not going to reply. Dane found he could not watch the visa plate now, Rip's hands about their task filled his whole range of sight.

He knew that Shannon was using every bit of his skill and

knowledge to jockey them into the position where they could ride their tail rockets down to the scorched rock of the E-Stat field. Perhaps it wasn't as smooth a landing as Jellico could have made. But they did it. Rip's hands were quiet, again that patch of darkness showed on the back of his tunic. He made no move from his seat.

"Secure—" Ali's voice floated up to them.

Dane unbuckled his safety webbing and got up, looking to Shannon for orders. This was Rip's plan they were to carry through. Then something moved him to give honor where it was due. He touched that bowed shoulder before him.

"Fin landing, brother! Four points and down!"

Rip glanced up, a grin made him look his old self. "Ought to have a recording of that for the Board when I go up for my pass-through."

Dane matched his smile. "Too bad we didn't have someone out there with a tri-dee machine."

"More likely it'd be evidence at our trial for piracy—" their words must have reached Ali on the ship's inter-com, for his deflating reply came back, to remind them of why they had made that particular landing. "Do we move now?"

"Check first," Rip said into the mike.

Dane looked at the visa-plate. Against a background of jagged rock teeth was the bubble of the E-Stat housing—more than three-quarters of it being in the hollowed out sections below the surface of the miniature world which supported it, as Dane knew. But a beam of light shown from the dome to center on the grounded Queen. They had not caught the Stat agents napping.

They made the rounds of the spacer, checking on each of the semi-conscious men. Ali had ready the artificial oxgy tanks —they must move fast once they began the actual task of clearing and restocking the hydro.

"Hope you have a good story ready," he commented as the other three joined him by the hatch to don the suits which would enable them to cross the airless, heatless surface of the asteroid.

"We have a poisoned hydro," Dane said.

"One look at the plants we dump will give you the lie. They won't accept our story without investigation."

Dane was aroused. Did Ali think he was as stupid as all that? "If you'd take a look in there now you'd believe me," he snapped.

"What did you do?" Ali sounded genuinely interested.

"Chucked a heated can of lacoil over a good section. It's wilting down fast in big patches."

Rip snorted. "Good old lacoil. You drink it, you wash in it, and now you kill off the Hydro with it. Maybe we can give the company an extra testimonial for the official jabber and collect when we hit Terra. All right—Weeks," he spoke to the little man, "you listen in on the com—it's tuned to our helmet units. We'll climb into these pipe suits and see how many tears we can wring out of the Eysies with our sad, sad tale."

They got into the awkward, bulky suits and squeezed into the hatch while Weeks slammed the lock door at their backs and operated the outer opening. Then they were looking out across the ground, still showing signs of the heat of their landing, and lighted by the dome beam.

"Nobody hurrying out with an aid and comfort kit," Rip's voice sounded in Dane's earphones. "A little slack aren't they?"

Slack—or was it that the Eysies had recognized the Queen and was preparing the sort of welcome the remnant of her crew could not withstand? Dane, wanting very much in his heart to be elsewhere, climbed down the ladder in Rip's wake, both of them spotlighted by the immovable beam from the Stat dome.

chapter 11

DESPERATE MEASURES

Measured in distance and time that rough walk in the ponderous suits across the broken terrain of the asteroid was a short one, measured by the beating of his own heart, Dane thought it much too long. There was no sign of life by the air lock of the bubble—no move on the part of the men stationed there to come to their assistance.

"D'you suppose we're invisible?" Ali's disembodied voice clicked in the helmet earphones.

"Maybe we'll wish we were," Dane could not forego that return.

Rip was almost to the air lock door now. His massively suited arm was outstretched toward the control bar when the com-unit in all three helmets caught the same demand:

"Identify!" The crisp order had enough snap to warn them that an answer was the best policy.

"Shannon—A-A of the Polestar," Rip gave the required information. "We claim E rights—"

But would they get them? Dane wondered. There was a click loud in his ears. The metal door was yielding to Rip's hand. At least those on the inside had taken off the lock. Dane quickened pace to join his leader.

Together the three from the Queen crowded through the lock door, saw that swing shut and seal behind them, as they stood waiting for the moment they could discard the suits and enter the dome. The odds against them could not be too high, this was a small Stat. It would not house more than four agents at the most. And they were familiar enough with the basic architecture of such stations to know just what move to make. Ali was to go to the com room where he could take over if they did meet with trouble. Dane and Rip would have to handle any dissenters in the main section. But they still hoped that luck might ride their fins and they could put over a story which would keep them out of active conflict with the Eysies.

The gauge on the wall registered safety and they unfastened, the protective clasps of the suits. Standing the cumbersome things against the wall as the inner door to the lock rolled back, they walked into Eysie territory.

As Free Traders they had the advantage of being uniformly tunicked—with no Company badge to betray their ship or status. So that could well *be* the "Polestar" standing needle slim behind them—and not the notorious "Solar Queen." But each, as he passed through the inner lock, gave a hitch to his belt which brought the butt of his sleep rod closer to hand. Innocuous as that weapon was, in close quarters its affect, if only temporary, was to some purpose. And since they were prepared for trouble, they might have a slight edge over the Eysies in attack.

A Company man, his tunic shabby and open in a negligent fashion at his thick throat, stood waiting for them. His unhelmeted head was grizzled, his coarse, tanned face with heavy jowls bristly enough to suggest he had not bothered to use smooth-cream for some days. An under officer of some spacer, retired to finish out the few years before pension in this nominal duty—fast letting down the standards of personal regime he had had to maintain on ship board. But he wasn't all fat and soft living, the glance with which he measured them was shrewdly appraising.

"What's your trouble?" he demanded without greeting. "You didn't I-dent coming in."

"Coms are out," Rip replied as shortly. "We need E-Hydro—"

"First time I ever heard it that the coms were wired in with the grass," the Eysies's hands were on his hips—in close proximity to something which made Dane's eyes narrow. The fellow was wearing a flare-blaster! That might be regulation equipment for an E-Stat agent on a lonely asteroid—but he didn't quite believe it. And probably the other was quick on the draw too.

"The coms are something else," Rip answered readily. "Our tech is working on them. But the hydro's bad all through. We'll have to dump and restock. Give you a voucher on Terra for the stuff."

The Eysie agent continued to block the doorway into the station. "This is private—I-S property. You should hit the Patrol post—they cater to you F-Ts."

"We hit the nearest E-Stat when we discovered that we were contaminated," Rip spoke with an assumption of patience. "That's the law, and you know it. You have to supply us and take a voucher—"

"How do I know that your voucher is worth the film it's recorded on?" asked the agent reasonably.

"All right," Rip shrugged. "If we have to do it the hard way, we'll cargo dump to cover your bill."

"Not on this field." The other shook his head. "I'll flash in your voucher first."

He had them, Dane thought bitterly. Their luck had run out. Because what he was going to do was a move they dared not protest. It was one any canny agent would make in the present situation. And if they were what they said they were, they must readily agree to let him flash their voucher of payment to I-S headquarters, to be checked and okayed before they took the hydro stock.

But Rip merely registered a mild resignation. "You the Com-tech? Where's your unit? I'll indit at once if you want it that way."

Whether their readiness to co-operate allayed some of the agent's suspicion or not, he relaxed some, giving them one more stare all around before he turned on his heel. "This way." They followed him down the narrow hall, Rip on his heels, the others behind.

"Lonely post," Rip commented. "I'd think you boys'd get space-whirly out here."

The other snorted. "We're not star lovers. And the pay's worth a three month stretch. They take us down for Terra leave before we start talking to the Whisperers."

"How many of you here at a time?" Rip edged the question in casually.

But the other might have been expecting it by the way he avoided giving a direct answer. "Enough to run the place— and not enough to help you clean out your wagon," he was short about it. "Any dumping you do is strictly on your own. You've enough hands on a spacer that size to manage—"

Rip laughed. "Far be it from me to ask an Eysie to do any real work," was his counter. "We know all about you Company men—"

But the agent did not take fire at that jib. Instead he pushed back a panel and they were looking into com-unit room where another man in the tunic of the I-S lounged on what was by law twenty-four hour duty, divided into three watches.

"These F-Ts want to flash a voucher request through," their guide informed the tech. The other, interested, gave them a searching once-over before he pushed a small scriber toward Rip.

"It's all yours—clear ether," he reported.

Ali stood with his back to the wall and Dane still lingered in the portal. Both of them fixed their attention on Rip's left hand. If he gave the agreed upon signal! Their fingers were linked loosely in their belts only an inch or so from their sleep rods.

With his right hand Rip scooped up the scribbler while the Com-tech half turned to make adjustments to the controls, picking up a speaker to call the I-S headquarters.

Rip's left index finger snapped across his thumb to form a circle. Ali's rod did not even leave his belt, it tilted up and the invisible deadening stream from it centered upon the seated tech. At the same instant Dane shot at the agent who had guided them there. The latter had time for a surprised grunt and his hand was at his blaster as he sagged to his knees and then relaxed on the floor. The Tech slumped across the call board as if sleep had overtaken him at his post.

Rip crossed the room and snapped off the switch which opened the wire for broadcasting. While Ali, with Dane's help, quietly and effectively immobilized the Eysies with their own belts.

"There should be at least three men here," Rip waited by the door. "We have to get them all under control before we start work."

However the interior of the bubble, extending as it did on levels beneath the outer crust of the asteroid, was not an easy place to search. An enemy, warned of the invasion, could easily keep ahead of the party from the Queen, spying on them at his leisure or preparing traps for them. In the end, afraid of wasting time, they contented themselves with locking the doors of the corridor leading to the lower levels, making ready to raid the storeroom they had discovered during their search.

Emergency hydro supplies consisted mainly of algae which could be stored in tanks and hastily put to use—as the plants now in the Queen took much longer to grow even under forcing methods. Dane volunteered to remain inside the E-Stat and assemble the necessary containers at the air lock while the other two, having had more experience, went back to the spacer to strip the hydro and prepare to switch contents.

But, when Rip and Ali left, the younger Cargo-apprentice

began to find the bubble a haunted place. He took the sealed containers out of their storage racks, stood them on a small hand truck, and pushed them to the foot of the stairs, up which he then climbed carrying two of the cylinders at a time.

The swish of the air current through the narrow corridors made a constant murmur of sound, but he found himself listening for something else, for a footfall other than his own, for the betraying rasp of clothing against a wall—for even a whisper of voice. And time and time again he paused suddenly to listen—sure that the faintest hint of such a sound had reached his ears. He had a dozen containers lined up when the welcome signal reached him by the con-unit of his field helmet. To transfer the cylinders to the lock, get out, and then open the outer door, did not take long. But as he waited he still listened for a sound which did not come—the notice that someone besides himself was free to move about the Stat.

Not knowing just how many of the supply tins were needed, he worked on transferring all there were in the storage racks to the upper corridor and the lock. But he still had half a dozen left to pass through when Rip sent a message that he was coming in.

Out of his pressure suit, the Astrogator-apprentice stepped lightly into the corridor, looked at the array of containers and shook his head.

"We don't need all those. No, leave them—" he added as Dane, with a sigh, started to pick up two for a return trip. "There's something more important just now—" He turned into the side hall which led to the com room.

Both the I-S men had awakened. The Com-tech appeared to accept his bonds philosophically. He was quiet and flat on his back, staring pensively at the ceiling. But the other agent had made a worm's progress half across the room and Rip had to halt in haste to prevent stepping on him.

Shannon stooped and, hooking his fingers in the other's tunic, heaved him back while the helpless man favored them

with some of the ripest speech—and NOT Trade Lingo—Dane
had ever heard. Rip waited until the man began to run down
and then he broke in with his pleasant soft drawl.

"Oh, sure, we're all that. But time runs on, Eysie, and I'd
like a couple of answers which may mean something to you.
First—when do you expect your relief?"

That set the agent off again. And his remarks—edited—were
that no something, something F-T was going to get any something, something information out of him!

But it was his companion in misfortune—the Com-tech—
who guessed the reason behind Rip's question.

"Cut jets!" he advised the other. "They're just being soft-
hearted. I take it," he spoke over the other agent's sputtering
to Rip, "that you're worried about leaving us fin down— That's
it, isn't it?"

Rip nodded. "In spite of what you think about us," he
replied, "We're not Patrol Posted outlaws—"

"No, you're just from a plague ship," the Com-tech remarked calmly. And his words struck his comrade dumb.
"Solar Queen?"

"You got the warn-off then?"

"Who didn't? You really have plague on board?" The
thought did not appear to alarm the Com-tech unduly. But
his fellow suddenly heaved his bound body some distance
away from the Free Traders and his face displayed mixed
emotions—most of them fearful.

"We have something—probably supplied," Rip straightened.
"Might pass along to your bosses that we know that. Now
suppose you tell me about your relief. When is it due?"

"Not until after we take off on the Long Orbit if you
leave us like this. On the other hand," the other added coolly,
"I don't see how you can do otherwise. We've still got those—"
with his chin he pointed to the com-unit.

"After a few alterations," Rip amended. The bulk of the
com was in a tightly sealed case which they would need a
flamer to open. But he could and did wreck havoc with the
exposed portions. The tech watching this distruction spouted

at least two expressions his companion had not used. But when Rip finished he was his unruffled self again.

"Now," Rip drew his sleep rod. "A little rest and when you wake it will all be a bad dream." He carefully beamed each man into slumber and helped Dane strip off their bonds. But before he left the room he placed on the recorder the voucher for the supplies they had taken. The Queen was not stealing—under the law she still had some shadow of rights.

Suited they crossed the rough rock to the ship. And there about the fins, already frozen into brittle spikes was a tangle of plants—the rich result of years of collecting.

"Did you find anything?" Dane asked as they rounded that mess on their way to the ladder.

Rip's voice came back through the helmit com. "Nothing we know how to interpret. I wish Frank or Craig had had a chance to check. We took tri-dees of everything before we dumped. Maybe they can learn something from these when—"

His voice trailed off leaving that "when" to ring in both their minds. It was such an important "when." When *would* either the steward or the Medic recover enough to view those tri-dee shots? Or was that "when" really an ominous "if?"

Back in the Queen, sealed once more for blast-off, they took their stations. Dane speculated as to the course Rip had set—were they just going to wander about the system hoping to escape notice until they had somehow solved their problem? Or did Shannon have some definite port in mind? He did not have time to ask before they lifted. But once they were space borne again he voiced his question.

Rip's face was serious. "Frankly—" he began and then hesitated for a long moment before he added, "I don't know. If we can only get the Captain or Craig on their feet again—"

"One thing," Ali materialized to join them, "Sinbad's back in the hydro. And this morning you couldn't get him inside the door. It's not a very good piece of evidence—"

No, it wasn't but they clung to it as backing for their actions of the past few hours. The cat that had shown such a marked distaste for the company of the stricken, and then for the hydro, was now content to visit the latter as if some evil he has sensed there had been cleansed with the dumping of the garden. They had not yet solved their mystery but another clue had come into their hands.

But now the care of the sick occupied hours and Rip insisted that a watch be maintained by the com—listening in for news which might concern the Queen. They had done a good job at silencing the E-Stat, for they had been almost six hours in space before the news of their raid was beamed to the nearest Patrol post.

Ali laughed. "Told you we'd be pirates," he said when he listened to that account of their descent upon the I-S station. "Though I didn't see all that blaster work they're now raving about. You'd think we fought a major battle there!"

Weeks growled. "The Eysies are trying to make it look good. Make us into outlaws—"

But Rip did not share in the general amusement at the wild extravagation of the report from the ether. "I notice they didn't say anything about the voucher we left."

Ali's cynical smile curled. "Did you expect them to? The Eysies think they have us by the tail fins now—why should they give us any benefit of the doubt? We junked all our boosters behind us on this take-off, and don't forget that, my friends."

Weeks looked confused. "But I thought you said we could do this legal," he appealed to Rip. "If we're Patrol Posted as outlaws—"

"They can't do any more to us than they can for running in a plague ship," Ali pointed out. "Either will get us blasted if we happen into the wrong vector now. So—what do we do?"

"We find out what the plague really is," Dane said and meant every word of it.

"How?" Ali inquired. "Through some of Craig's magic?"

Dane was forced to answer with the truth. "I don't know yet —but it's our only chance."

Rip rubbed his eyes wearily. "Don't think I'm disagreeing —but just where do we start? We've already combed Frank's quarters and Kosti's—we cleaned out the hydro—"

"Those tri-dee shots of the hydro—have you checked them yet?" Dane countered.

Without a word Ali arose and left the cabin. He came back with a microfilm roll. Fitting it into the large projector he focused it on the wall and snapped the button.

They were looking at the hydro—down the length of space so accurately recorded that it seemed they might walk straight into it. The greenery of the plants was so vivid and alive Dane felt that he could reach out and pluck a leaf. Inch by inch he examined those ranks, looking for something which was not in order, had no right to be there.

The long shot of the hydro as it had been merged into a series of sectional groupings. In silence they studied it intently, using all their field lore in an attempt to spot what each one was certain must be there somewhere. But they were all handicapped by their lack of intimate knowledge of the garden.

"Wait!" Weeks' voice scaled up. "Left hand corner—there!" His pointing hand broke and shadowed the portion he was calling to their attention. Ali jumped to the projector and made a quick adjustment.

Plants four and five times life size glowed green on the wall. What Weeks had caught they all saw now—ragged leaves, stripped stems.

"Chewed!" Dane supplied the answer.

It was only one species of plant which had been so mangled. Other varieties in the same bank showed no signs of disturbance. But all of that one type had at least one stripped branch and two were virtual skeletons.

"A pest!" said Rip.

"But Sinbad," Dane began a protest before the memory of the cat's peculiar actions of the past weeks stopped him. Sinbad had slipped up, the hunter who had kept the Queen free of the outré alien life which came aboard from time to time with cargo, had not attacked that which had ravaged the hydro plants. Or if he had done so, he had not, after his usual custom, presented the bodies of the slain to any crew member.

"It looks as if we have something at last," Ali observed and someone echoed that with a sigh of heartdeep relief.

chapter 12

STRANGE BEHAVIOR
OF A HOOBAT

"All right, so we think we know a little more," Ali added a moment later. "Just what are we going to do? We can't stay in space forever—there're the small items of fuel and supplies and—"

Rip had come to a decision. "We're not going to remain space borne," he stated with the confidence of one who now saw an open road before him.

"Luna—" Weeks was plainly doubtful.

"No. Not after that warn-off. Terra!"

For a second or two the other three stared at Rip agape. The audacity and danger of what he suggested was a little stunning. Since men had taken regularly to space no ship had made a direct landing on their home planet—all had passed through the quarantine on Luna. It was not only risky—it was so unheard of that for some minutes they did not understand him.

"We try to set down at Terraport," Dane found his tongue first, "and they flame us out—"

Rip was smiling. "The trouble with you," he addressed them all, "is that you think of earth only in terms of Terraport—"

"Well, there *is* the Patrol field at Stella," Weeks agreed doubtfully. "But we'd be right in the middle of trouble there—"

"Did we have a regular port on Sargol—on Limbo—on fifty others I can name out of our log?" Rip wanted to know.

Ali voiced a new objection. "So—we have the luck of Jones and we set down somewhere out of sight. Then what do we do?"

"We seal ship until we find the pest—then we bring in a Medic and get to the bottom of the whole thing," Rip's confidence was contagious. Dane almost believed that it *could* be done that way.

"Did you ever think," Ali cut in, "what would happen if we were wrong—if the Queen really is a plague carrier?"

"I said—we seal the ship—tight," countered Shannon. "And when we earth it'll be where we won't have visitors to infect—"

"And that is where?" Ali, who knew the deserts of Mars better than he did the greener planet from which his stock had sprung, pursued the question.

"Right in the middle of the Big Burn!"

Dane, Terra born and bred, realized first what Rip was planning and what it meant. Sealed off was right—the Queen would be amply protected from investigation. Whether her crew would survive was another matter—whether she could even make a landing there was also to be considered.

The Big Burn was the horrible scar left by the last of the Atomic Wars—a section of radiation poisoned land comprising hundreds of square miles—land which generations had never dared to penetrate. Originally the survivors of that war had shunned the whole continent which it disfigured. It had been close to two centuries before men had gone into the still wholesome land laying to the far west and the south. And, through the years, the avoidance of the Big Burn had become part of their racial instinct so they shrank from it. It was a symbol of something no Terran wanted to remember.

But Ali now had only one question to ask. "Can we do it?"

"We'll never know until we try," was Rip's reply.

"The Patrol'll be watching—" that was Weeks. With his Venusian background he had less respect for the dangers of the Big Burn than he did for the forces of Law and order which ranged the star lanes.

"They'll be watching the routine lanes," Rip pointed out. "They won't expect a ship to come in on that vector, steering away from the ports. Why should they? As far as I know it's never been tried since Terraport was laid out. It'll be tricky—" And he himself would have to bear most of the responsibility for it. "But I believe that it can be done. And we can't just roam around out here. With I-S out for our blood and a Patrol warn-off it won't do us any good to head for Luna—"

None of his listeners could argue with that. And, Dane's spirits began to rise, after all they knew so little about the Big Burn—it might afford them just the temporary sanctuary they needed. In the end they agreed to try it, mainly because none of them could see any alternative, except the too dangerous one of trying to contact the authorities and being summarily treated as a plague ship before they could defend themselves.

And their decision was ably endorsed not long afterwards by a sardonic warning on the com—a warning which Ali who had been tending the machine passed along to them.

"Greetings, pirates—"

"What do you mean?" Dane was heating broth to feed to Captain Jellico.

"The word has gone out—our raid on the E-Stat is now a matter of history and Patrol record—we've been Posted!"

Dane felt a cold finger drawn along his backbone. Now they were fair game for the whole system. Any Patrol ship that wanted could shoot them down with no questions asked. Of course that had always been a possibility from the first after their raid on the E-Stat. But to realize that it was now true was a different matter altogether. This was one occasion when realization was worse than anticipation. He tried to keep his voice level as he answered:

"Let us hope we can pull off Rip's plan—"

"We'd better. What about the Big Burn anyway, Thorson? Is it as tough as the stories say?"

"We don't know what it's like. It's never been explored—or at least those who tried to explore its interior never reported in afterwards. As far as I know it's left strictly alone."

"Is it still all 'hot'?"

"Parts of it must be. But all—we don't know."

With the bottle of soup in his hand Dane climbed to Jellico's cabin. And he was so occupied with the problem at hand that at first he did not see what was happening in the small room. He had braced the Captain up into a half-sitting position and was patiently ladling the liquid into his mouth a spoonful at a time when a thin squeak drew his attention to the top of Jellico's desk.

From the half open lid of a microtape compartment something long and dark projected, beating the air feebly. Dane, easing the Captain back on the bunk, was going to investigate when the Hoobat broke its unnatural quiet of the past few days with an ear-splitting screech of fury. Dane struck at the bottom of its cage—the move its master always used to silence it— But this time the results were spectacular.

The cage bounced up and down on the spring which secured it to the ceiling of the cabin and the blue feathered horror slammed against the wires. Either its clawing had weakened them, or some fault had developed, for they parted and the Hoobat came through them to land with a sullen plop on the desk. Its screams stopped as suddenly as they had begun and it scuttled on its spider-toad legs to the microtape compartment, acting with purposeful dispatch and paying no attention to Dane.

Its claws shot out and with ease it extracted from the compartment a creature as weird as itself—one which came fighting and of which Dane could not get a very clear idea. Struggling they battled across the surface of the desk and flopped to the floor. There the hunted broke loose from the hunter and fled with fantastic speed into the corridor. And before Dane could move the Hoobat was after it.

He gained the passage just in time to see Queex disappear down the ladder, climbing with the aid of its pincher claws, apparently grimly determined to catch up with the thing it pursued. And Dane went after them.

There was no sign of the creature who fled on the next level. But Dane made no move to recapture the blue hunter who squatted at the foot of the ladder staring unblinkingly into space. Dane waited, afraid to disturb the Hoobat. He had not had a good look at the thing which had run from Queex— but he knew that it was something which had no business aboard the Queen. And it might be the disturbing factor they were searching for. If the Hoobat would only lead him to it—

The Hoobat moved, rearing up on the tips of its six legs, its neckless head slowly revolving on its puffy shoulders. Along the ridge of its backbone its blue feathers were rising into a crest much as Sinbad's fur rose when the cat was afraid or angry. Then, without any sign of haste, it crawled over and began descending the ladder once more, heading toward the lower section which housed the Hydro.

Dane remained where he was until it had almost reached the deck of the next level and then he followed, one step at a time. He was sure that the Hoobat's peculiar construction of body prevented it from looking up—unless it turned upon its back—but he did not want to do anything which would alarm it or deter Queex from what he was sure was a methodical chase.

Queex stopped again at the foot of the second descent and sat in its toad stance, apparently brooding, a round blue blot. Dane clung to the ladder and prayed that no one would happen along to frighten it. Then, just as he was beginning to wonder if it had lost contact with its prey, once more it arose and with the same speed it had displayed in the Captain's cabin it shot along the corridor to the hydro.

To Dane's knowledge the door of the garden was not only shut but sealed. And how either the stranger or Queex could get through it he did not see.

"What the—?" Ali clattered down the ladder to halt abruptly as Dane waved at him.

"Queex," the Cargo-apprentice kept his voice to a half whisper, "it got loose and chased something out of the Old Man's cabin down here."

"Queex—!" Ali began and then shut his mouth, moving noiselessly up to join Dane.

The short corridor ended at the hydro entrance. And Dane had been right, there they found the Hoobat, crouched at the closed panel, its claws clicking against the metal as it picked away uselessly at the portal which would not admit it.

"What ever it's after must be in there," Dane said softly.

And the hydro, stripped of its luxuriance of plant life, occupied now by the tanks of green scum, would not afford too many hiding places. They had only to let Queex in and keep watch.

As they came up the Hoobat flattened to the floor and shrilled its war cry, spitting at their boots and then flashing claws against the stout metal enforced hide. However, though it was prepared to fight them, it showed no signs of wishing to retreat, and for that Dane was thankful. He quickly pressed the release and tugged open the panel.

At the first crack of its opening Queex turned with one of those bursts of astounding speed and clawed for admittance, its protest against the men forgotten. And it squeezed through a space Dane would have thought too narrow to accommodate its bloated body. Both men slipped around the door behind it and closed the panel tight.

The air was not as fresh as it had been when the plants were there. And the vats which had taken the places of the banked greenery were certainly nothing to look at. Queex humped itself into a clod of blue, immovable, halfway down the aisle.

Dane tried to subdue his breathing, to listen. The Hoobat's actions certainly argued that the alien thing had taken refuge here, though how it had gotten through—? But if it were in the hydro it was well hidden.

He had just begun to wonder how long they must wait when Queex again went into action. Its clawed front legs upraised, it brought the pinchers deliberately together and sawed one across the other, producing a rasping sound which was almost a vibration in the air. Back and forth, back and forth, moved the claws. Watching them produced almost a hypnotic affect, and the reason for such a maneuver was totally beyond the human watchers.

But Queex knew what it was doing all right, Ali's fingers closed on Dane's arm in a pincher grip as painful as if he had been equipped with the horny armament of the Hoobat.

Something, a flitting shadow, had rounded one vat and was that much closer to the industrious fiddler on the floor. By some weird magic of its own the Hoobat was calling its prey to it.

Scrape, scrape—the unmusical performance continued with monotonous regularity. Again the shadow flashed—one vat closer. The Hoobat now presented the appearance of one charmed by its own art—sunk in a lethargy of weird music making.

At last the enchanted came into full view, though lingering at the round side of a container, very apparently longing to flee again, but under some compulsion to approach its enchanter. Dane blinked, not quite sure that his eyes were not playing tricks on him. He had seen the almost transparent globe "bogies" of Limbo, had been fascinated by the weird and ugly pictures in Captain Jellico's collection of tri-dee prints. But this creature was as impossible in its way as the horrific blue thing dragging it out of concealment.

It walked erect on two threads of legs, with four knobby joints easily detected. A bulging abdomen sheathed in the norny substance of a beetle's shell ended in a sharp point. Two pairs of small legs, folded close to the much smaller upper portion of its body, were equipped with thorn sharp terminations. The head, which constantly turned back and forth on the armor plated shoulders, was long and narrow and split for half its length by a mouth above which were deep pits which must harbor eyes, though actual organs were not visible to the watching men. It was a palish gray in color —which surprised Dane a little. His memory of the few seconds he had seen it on the Captain's desk had suggested that it was much darker. And erect as it was, it stood about eighteen inches high.

With head turning rapidly, it still hesitated by the side of the vat, so nearly the color of the metal that unless it moved it was difficult to distinguish. As far as Dane could see the Hoobat was paying it no attention. Queex might be lost in a happy dream, the result of its own fiddling. Nor did the rhythm of that scrapping vary.

The nightmare thing made the last foot in a rush of speed which reduced it to a blur, coming to a halt before the Hoobat. Its front legs whipped out to strike at its enemy. But Queex was no longer dreaming. This was the moment the Hoobat had been awaiting. One of the sawing claws opened and closed, separating the head of the lurker from its body. And before either of the men could interfere Queex had dismembered the prey with dispatch.

"Look there!" Dane pointed.

The Hoobat held close the body of the stranger and where the ashy corpse came into contact with Queex's blue feathered skin it was slowly changing hue—as if some of the color of its hunter had rubbed off on it.

"Chameleon!" Ali went down on one knee the better to view the grisly feast now in progress. "Watch out!" he added sharply as Dane came to join him.

One of the thin upper limbs lay where Queex had discarded it. And from the needle tip was oozing some colorless drops of fluid. Poison?

Dane looked around for something which he could use to pick up the still jerking appendage. But before he could find anything Queex had appropriated it. And in the end they had to allow the Hoobat its victim in its entirety. But once Queex had consumed its prey it lapsed into its usual hunched immobility. Dane went for the cage and working gingerly he and Ali got the creature back in captivity. But all the evidence now left were some smears on the floor of the hydro, smears which Ali blotted up for future research in the lab.

An hour later the four who now comprised the crew of the Queen gathered in the mess for a conference. Queex was in its cage on the table before them, asleep after all its untoward activity.

"There must be more than just one," Weeks said. "But how are we going to hunt them down? With Sinbad?"

Dane shook his head. Once the Hoobat had been caged and the more prominent evidence of the battle scrapped from the floor, he had brought the cat into the hydro and forced him to sniff at the site of the engagement. The result was that Sinbad had gone raving mad and Dane's hands were now covered with claw tears which ran viciously deep. It was plain that the ship's cat was having none of the intruders, alive or dead. He had fled to Dane's cabin where he had taken refuge on the bunk and snarled wild eyed when anyone looked in from the corridor.

"Queex has to do it," Rip said. "But will it hunt unless it is hungry?"

He surveyed the now comatose creature skeptically. They had never seen the Captain's pet eat anything except some pellets which Jellico kept in his desk, and they were aware that the intervals between such feedings were quite lengthy. If they had to wait the usual time for Queex to feel hunger pangs once more, they might have to wait a long time.

"We should catch one alive," Ali remarked thoughtfully. "If we could get Queex to fiddle it out to where we could net it—"

Weeks nodded eagerly. "A small net like those the Salariki use. Drop it over the thing—"

While Queex still drowsed in its cage Weeks went to work with fine cord. Holding the color changing abilities of the enemy in mind they could not tell how many of the creatures might be roaming the ship. It could only be proved where they *weren't* by where Sinbad would consent to stay. So they made plans which included both the cat and the Hoobat.

Sinbad, much against his will, was buckled into an improvised harness by which he could be controlled without the handler losing too much valuable skin.

And then the hunt started at the top of the ship, proceeding downward section by section. Sinbad raised no protest in the control cabin, nor in the private cabins of the officers' thereabouts. If they could interpret his reactions the center section was free of the invaders. So with Dane in control of the cat and Ali carrying the caged Hoobat, they descended once more to the level which housed the hydro, galley, steward's quarters and ship's sick bay.

Sinbad proceeded on his own four feet into the galley and the mess. He was not uneasy in the sick bay, nor in Mura's cabin, and this time he even paced the hydro without being dragged—much to their surprise as they had thought that the headquarters of the stowaways.

"Could there only have been one?" Weeks wanted to know as he stood by ready with the net in his hands.

"Either that—or else we're wrong about the hydro being their main hideout. If they're afraid of Queex now they may have withdrawn to the place they feel the safest," Rip said.

It was when they were on the ladder leading to the cargo level that Sinbad balked. He planted himself firmly and yowled against further progress until Dane, with the harness, pulled him along.

"Look at Queex!"

They followed Weeks' order. The Hoobat was no longer lethargic. It was raising itself, leaning forward to clasp the bars of its cage, and now it uttered one of its screams of rage. And as Ali went on down the ladder it rattled the bars in a determined effort for freedom. Sinbad, spitting and yowling refused to walk. Rip nodded to Ali.

"Let it out."

Tipped out of its cage the Hoobat scuttled forward, straight for the panel which opened on the large cargo space and there waited, as if for them to open the portal and admit the hunter to its hunting territory.

chapter 13

OFF THE MAP

Across the lock of the panel was the seal set in place by Van Rycke before the spacer had lifted from Sargol. Under Dane's inspection it showed no crack. To all evidences the hatch had not been opened since they left the perfumed planet. And yet the hunting Hoobat was sure that the invading pests were within.

It took only a second for Dane to commit an act which, if he could not defend it later, would blacklist him out of space. He twisted off the official seal which should remain there while the frighter was space borne.

With Ali's help he shouldered aside the heavy sliding panel and they looked into the cargo space, now filled with the red wood from Sargol. The red wood! When he saw it Dane was struck with their stupidity. Aside from the Koros stones in the stone box, only the wood had come from the Salariki world. What if the pests had not been planted by I-S agents, but were natives of Sargol being brought in with the wood?

The men remained at the hatch to allow the Hoobat freedom in its hunt. And Sinbad crouched behind them, snarling and giving voice to a rumbling growl which was his negative opinion of the proceedings.

They were conscious of an odor—the sharp, unidentifiable-scent Dane had noticed during the loading of the wood. It was not unpleasant—merely different. And if—or something—had an electrifying effect upon Queex. The blue hunter climbed with the aid of its claws to the top of the nearest pile of wood and there settled down. For a space it was apparently contemplating the area about it.

Then it raised its claws and began the scrapping fiddle which once before had drawn its prey out of hiding. Oddly enough that dry rasp of sound had a quieting effect upon Sinbad and Dane felt the drag of the harness lessen as the cat moved, not toward escape, but to the scene of action, humping himself at last in the open panel, his round eyes fixed upon the Hoobat with a fascinated stare.

Scrape-scrape—the monotonous noise bit into the ears of the men, gnawed at their nerves.

"Ahhh—" Ali kept his voice to a whisper, but his hand jerked to draw their attention to the right at deck level. Dane saw that flicker along a log. The stowaway pest was now the same brilliant color as the wood, indistinguishable until it moved, which probably explained how it had come on board.

But that was only the first arrival. A second flash of movement and a third followed. Then the hunted remained stationary, able to resist for a period the insidious summoning of Queex. The Hoobat maintained an attitude of indifference, of being so wrapped in its music making that nothing else existed. Rip whispered to Weeks:

"There's one to the left—on the very end of that log. Can you net it?"

The small oiler slipped the coiled mesh through his calloused hands. He edged around Ali, keeping his eyes on the protruding bump of red upon red which was his quarry.

"—two—three—four—five—" Ali was counting under his

breath but Dane could not see that many. He was sure of only four, and those because he had seen them move.

The things were ringing in the pile of wood where the Hoobat fiddled, and two had ascended the first logs toward their doom. Weeks went down on one knee, ready to cast his net, when Dane had his first inspiration. He drew his sleep rod, easing it out of its holster, set the lever on "spray" and beamed it at three of those humps.

Rip seeing what he was doing, dropped a hand on Weeks' shoulder, holding the oiler in check. A hump moved, slide down the rounded side of the log into the narrow aisle of deck between two piles of wood. It lay quiet, a bright scarlet blot against the gray.

Then Weeks did move, throwing his net over it and jerking the draw string tight, at the same time pulling the captive toward him over the deck. But, even as it came, the scarlet of the thing's body was fast fading to an ashy pink and at last taking on a gray as dull as the metal on which it lay—the complete camouflage. Had they not had it enmeshed they might have lost it altogether, so well did it now blend with the surface.

The other two in the path of the ray had not lost their grip upon the logs, and the men could not advance to scoop them up. Not while there were others not affected, free to flee back into hiding. Weeks bound the net about the captive and looked to Rip for orders.

"Deep freeze," the acting-commander of the Queen said succinctly. "Let me see it get out of that!"

Surely the cold of the deep freeze, united to the sleep ray, would keep the creature under control until they had a chance to study it. But, as Weeks passed Sinbad on his errand, the cat was so frantic to avoid him, that he reared up on his hind legs, almost turning a somersault, snarling and spitting until Weeks was up the ladder to the next level. It was very evident that the ship's cat was having none of this pest.

They might have been invisible and their actions non-existent as far as Queex was concerned. For the Hoobat continued its siren concert. The lured became more reckless, mounting the logs to Queex's post in sudden darts. Dane wondered how the Hoobat proposed handling four of the creatures at once. For, although the other two which had been in the path of the ray had not moved, he now counted four climbing.

"Stand by to ray—" that was Rip.

But it would have been interesting to see how Queex *was* prepared to handle the four. And, though Rip had given the order to stand by, he had not ordered the ray to be used. Was he, too, interested in that?

The first red projection was within a foot of the Hoobat now and its fellows had frozen as if to allow it the honor of battle with the feathered enemy. To all appearances Queex did did not see it, but when it sprang with a whir of speed which would baffle a human, the Hoobat was ready and its claws, halting their rasp, met around the wasp-thin waist of the pest, speedily cutting it in two. Only this time the Hoobat made no move to unjoint and consume the victim. Instead it squatted in utter silence, as motionless as a tri-dee print.

The heavy lower half of the creature rolled down the pile of logs to the deck and there paled to the gray of its background. None of its kind appeared to be interested in its fate. The two which had been in the path of the ray, continued to be humps on the wood, the others faced the Hoobat.

But Rip was ready to waste no more time. "Ray them!" he snapped.

All three of their sleep rods sprayed the pile, catching in passing the Hoobat. Queex's pop eyes closed, but it showed no other sign of falling under the spell of the beam.

Certain that all the creatures in sight were now relatively harmless, the three approached the logs. But it was necessary to get into touching distance before they could even make out the outlines of the nightmare things, so well did their protective coloring conceal them. Wearing gloves Ali detached the little monsters from their holds on the wood and put them for temporary safekeeping—during a transfer to the deep freeze— into the Hoobat's cage. Queex, they decided to leave where it was for a space, to awaken and trap any survivor which had been too wary to emerge at the first siren song. As far as they could tell the Hoobat was their only possible protection against the pest and to leave it in the center of infection was the wisest course.

Having dumped the now metal colored catch into the freeze, they held a conference.

"No plague—" Weeks breathed a sigh of relief.

"No proof of that yet," Ali caught him up short. "We have to prove it past any reasonable doubt."

"And how are we going to do—?" Dane began when he saw what the other had brought in from Tau's stores. A lancet and the upper half of the creature Queex had killed in the cargo hold.

The needle pointed front feet of the thing were curled up in its death throes and it was now a dirty white shade as if the ability to change color had been lost before it matched the cotton on which it lay. With the lancet Ali forced a claw away from the body. It was oozing the watery liquid which they had seen on the one in the hydro.

"I have an idea," he said slowly, his eyes on the mangled creature rather than on his shipmates, "that we might have escaped being attacked because they sheered off from us. But if we were clawed we might take it too. Remember those marks on the throats and backs of the rest? That might be the entry point of this poison—if poison it is—"

Dane could see the end of that line of reasoning. Rip and Ali—they couldn't be spared. The knowledge they had would bring the Queen to earth. But a Cargo-master was excess baggage when there was no reason for trade. It was his place to try out the truth of Ali's surmise.

But while he thought another acted. Weeks leaned over and twitched the lancet out of Ali's fingers. Then, before any of them could move, he thrust its contaminated point into the back of his hand.

"Don't!"

Both Dane's cry and Rip's hand came too late. It had been done. And Weeks sat there, looking alone and frightened, studying the drop of blood which marked the dig of the surgeon's keen knife. But when he spoke his voice sounded perfectly natural.

"Headache first, isn't it?"

Only Ali was outwardly unaffected by what the little man had just done. "Just be sure you have a real one," he warned with what Dane privately considered real callousness.

Weeks nodded. "Don't let my imagination work," he answered shrewdly. "I know. It has to be real. How long do you suppose?"

"We don't know," Rip sounded tired, beaten. "Meanwhile," he got to his feet, "we'd better set a course home—"

"Home," Weeks repeated. To him Terra was not his own home—he had been born in the polar swamps of Venus. But to all Solarians—no matter which planet had nurtured them—Terra was home.

"You," Rip's big hand fell gently on the little oiler's shoulder, "stay here with Thorson—"

"No," Weeks shook his head. "Unless I black out, I'm riding station in the engine room. Maybe the bug won't work on me anyway."

And because he had done what he had done they could not deny him the right to ride his station as long as he could during the grueling hours to come.

Dane visited the cargo hold once more. To be greeted by an irate scream which assured him that Queex was again awake and on guard. Although the Hoobat was ready enough to give tongue, it still squatted in its chosen position on top of the log stack and he did not try to dislodge it. Perhaps with Queex planted in the enemies' territory they would have nothing to fear from any pests not now confined in the deep freeze.

Rip set his course for Terra—for that plague spot on their native world where they might hide out the Queen until they could prove their point—that the spacer was not a disease ridden ship to be feared. He kept to the control cabin, shifting only between the Astrogator's and the pilot's station. Upon him alone rested the responsibility of bringing in the ship along a vector which crossed no well traveled space lane where the Patrol might challenge them. Dane rode out the orbiting in the Comtech's seat, listening in for the first warning of danger—that they had been detected.

The mechanical repetition of their list of crimes was now stale news and largely off-ether. And from all traces he could pick up, they were lost as far as the authorities were concerned. On the other hand, the Patrol might indeed be as far knowing as its propaganda stated and the Queen was running headlong into a trap. Only they had no choice in the matter.

It was the ship's inter-com bringing Ali's voice from the engine room which broke the concentration in the control cabin.

"Weeks' down!"

Rip barked into the mike: "How bad?"

"He hasn't blacked out yet. The pains in his head are pretty bad and his hand is swelling—"

"He's given us our proof. Tell him to report off—"

But the disembodied voice which answered that was Weeks'.

"I haven't got it as bad as the others. I'll ride this out."

Rip shook his head. But short-handed as they were he could not argue Weeks away from his post if the man insisted upon staying. He had other, and for the time being, more important matters before him.

How long they sweated out that descent upon their native world Dane could never afterwards have testified. He only knew that hours must have passed, until he thought groggily that he could not remember a time he was not glued in the seat which had been Tang's, the earphones pressing against his sweating skull, his fatigue-drugged mind being held with difficulty to the duty at hand.

Sometime during that haze they made their landing. He had a dim memory of Rip sprawled across the pilot's control board and then utter exhaustion claimed him also and the darkness closed in. When he roused it was to look about a cabin tilted to one side. Rip was still slumped in a muscle cramping posture, breathing heavily. Dane bit out a forceful word born of twinges of his own, and then snapped on the visa-plate.

For a long moment he was sure that he was not yet awake. And then, as his dazed mind supplied names for what he saw, he knew that Rip had failed. Far from being in the center— or at least well within the perimeter of the dread Big Burn— they must have landed in some civic park or national forest. For the massed green outside, the bright flowers, the bird he sighted as a brilliant flash of wind coasting color—those were not to be found in the twisted horror left by man's last attempt to impress his will upon his resisting kind.

Well, it had been a good try, but there was no use expecting luck to ride their fins all the way, and they had had more than their share in the E-Stat affair. How long would it be before the Law arrived to collect them? Would they have time to state their case?

The faint hope that they might aroused him. He reached for the com key and a second later tore the headphones from his appalled ears. The crackle of static he knew—and the numerous strange noises which broke in upon the lanes of communication in space—but this solid, paralyzing roar was something totally new—new, and frightening.

And because it was new and he could not account for it, he turned back to regard the scene on the viewer with a more critical eye. The foliage which grew in riotous profusion was green right enough, and Terra green into the bargain—there was no mistaking that. But—Dane caught at the edge of the Com-unit for support. But— What was that liver-red blossom which had just reached out to engulf a small flying thing?

Feverishly he tried to remember the little natural history he knew. Sure that what he had just witnessed was unnatural— un-Terran—and to be suspect!

He started the spy lens on its slow revolution in the Queen's nose, to get a full picture of their immediate surroundings. It was tilted at an angle—apparently they had *not* made a fin-point landing this time—and sometimes it merely reflected slices of sky. But when it swept earthward he saw enough to make him believe that wherever the spacer had set down it was not on the Terra he knew.

Subconsciously he had expected the Big Burn to be barren land—curdled rock with rivers of frozen quartz, substances boiled up through the crust of the planet by the action of the atomic explosives. That was the way it had been on Limbo— on the other "burned-off" worlds they had discovered where those who had proceeded mankind into the Galaxy—the mysterious, long vanished "Forerunners"—had fought their grim and totally annihilating wars.

But it would seem that the Big Burn was altogether different —at least here it was. There was no rock sterile of life outside —in fact there would appear to be too much life. What Dane could sight on his limited field of vision was a teeming jungle. And the thrill of that discovery almost made him forget their present circumstances. He was still staring bemused at the screen when Rip muttered, turned his head on his folded arms and opened his sunken eyes:

"Did we make it?" he asked dully.

Dane, not taking his eyes from that fascinating scene without, answered: "You brought us down. But I don't know where—"

"Unless our instruments were 'way off, we're near to the heart of the Burn."

"Some heart!"

"What does it look like?" Rip sounded too tired to cross the cabin and see for himself. "Barren as Limbo?"

"Hardly! Rip, did you ever see a tomato as big as a mellon— At least it looks like a tomato," Dane halted the spy lens as it focused upon this new phenomena.

"A what?" There was a note of concern in Shannon's voice. "What's the matter with you, Dane?"

"Come and see," Dane willingly yielded his place to Rip but he did not step out of range of the screen. Surely that did have the likeness to a good, old fashioned earthside tomato—but it was mellon size and it hung from a bush which was close to a ten foot tree!

Rip stumbled across to drop into the Com-tech's place.

But his expression of worry changed to one of simple astonishment as he saw that picture.

"Where are we?"

"You name it," Dane had had longer to adjust, the excitement of an explorer sighting virgin territory worked in his veins, banishing fatigue. "It must be the Big Burn!"

"But," Rip shook his head slowly as if with that gesture to deny the evidence before his eyes, "that country's all bare rock. I've seen pictures—"

"Of the outer rim," Dane corrected, having already solved that problem for himself. "This must be farther in than any survey ship ever came. Great. Spirit of Outer Space, what has happened here?"

Rip had enough technical training to know how to get part of the answer. He leaned halfway across the com, and was able to flick down a lever with the very tip of his longest finger. Instantly the cabin was filled with a clicking so loud as to make an almost continuous drone of sound.

Dane knew that danger signal, he didn't need Rip's words to underline it for him.

"That's what's happened. This country is pile 'hot' out there!"

chapter 14

SPECIAL MISSION

That click, the dial beneath the counter, warned them that they were as cut off from the luxuriance outside as if they were viewing a scene on Mars or Sargol from their present position. To go beyond the shielding walls of the spacer into that riotous green world would sentence them to death as surely as if the Patrol was without, with a flamer trained on their hatch. There was no escape from that radiation—it would be in the air one breathed, strike through one's skin. And yet the wilderness flourished and beckoned.

"Mutations—" Rip mused. "Space, Tau'd go wild if he could see it!"

And that mention of the Medic brought them back to the problem which had earthed them. Dane leaned back against the slanting wall of the cabin.

"We have to have a Medic—"

Rip nodded without looking away from the screen.

"Can one of the flitters be shielded?" The Cargo-apprentice persisted.

"That's a thought! Ali should how—" Rip reached for the inter-com mike. "Engines!"

"So you *are* alive?" Ali's voice had a bite in it. "About time you're contacting. Where are we? Besides being lopsided from a recruit's scrambled set-down, I mean."

"In the Big Burn. Come top-side. Wait—how's Weeks?"

"He has a devil's own headache, but he hasn't blacked out yet. Looks like his immunity holds in part. I've sent him bunk-side for a while with a couple of pain pills. So we've made it—"

He must have left to join them for when Rip answered: "After a fashion," into the mike there was no reply.

And the clang of his boot plates on the ladder heralded his arrival at their post. There was an interval for him to view the outer world and accept the verdict of the counter and then Rip voiced Dane's question:

"Can we shield one of the flitters well enough to cross that? I can't take the Queen up and earth her again—"

"I know you can't!" the acting-engineer cut in. "Maybe you could get her off world, but you'll come close to blasting out when you try for another landing. Fuel doesn't go on forever —though some of you space jockeys seem to think it does. The flitter? Well, we've some spare rocket linings. But it's going to be a job and a half to get those beaten out and reassembled. And, frankly, the space whirly one who flies her had better be suited and praying loudly when he takes off. We can always try—" He was frowning, already busied with the problem which was one for his department.

So with intervals of snatched sleep, hurried meals, and the time which must be given to tending their unconscious charges, Rip and Dane became only hands to be directed by Ali's brain and garnered knowledge. Weeks slept off the worst of his pain and, though he complained of weakness, he tottered back on duty to help.

The flitter—an air sled intended to hold three men and supplies for exploring trips on strange worlds—was first stripped of all non-essentials until what remained was not much more than the pilot's seat and the motor. Then they labored to build up a shielding of the tough radiation dulling alloy which was used to line rocket tubes. And they could only praise the fore-sight of Stotz who carried such a full supply of spare parts and tools. It was a task over which they often despaired, and Ali improvised frantically, performing weird adjustments of engineering structure. He was still unsatisfied when they had done.

"She'll fly," he admitted. "And she's the best we can do. But it'll depend a lot on how far she has to go over 'hot' country. Which way do we head her?"

Rip had been busy with a map of Terra—a small thing he had discovered in one of the travel recordings carried for crew entertainment.

"The Big Burn covers three quarters of this continent. There's no use going north—the devastated area extends into the arctic regions. I'd say west—there're some fringe settlements on the sea coast and we need to contact a frontier territory. Now do we have it straight—? I take the flitter, get a Medic and bring him back—"

Dane cut in at that point. "Correct course! You stay here. If the Queen has to lift, you're the only one who can take her off world. And the same's true for Ali. I can't ride out a blast-off in either the pilot's or the engineer's seat. And Weeks is on the sick list. So I'm elected to do the Medic hunting—"

They were forced to agree to that. He was no hero, Dane thought, as he gave a last glance about his cabin early the next morning. The small cubby, utilitarian and bare as it was, never looked more inviting or secure. No, no hero, it was merely a matter of common sense. And although his imagination—that deeply hidden imagination with which few of his fellows credited him—shrank from the ordeal ahead, he had not the slightest intention of allowing that to deter him.

The space suit, which had been bulky and clumsy enough on the E-Stat asteroid under limited gravity, was almost twice as poorly adapted to progression on earth. But he climbed into it with Rip's aid, while Ali lashed a second suit under the seat—ready to encase the man Dane must bring back with him. Before he closed the helmet, Rip had one last order to give, along with an unexpected piece of equipment. And, when Dane saw that, he knew just how desperate Shannon considered their situation to be. For only on life or death terms would the Astrogator-apprentice have used Jellico's private key, opened the forbidden arms cabinet, and withdrawn that blaster.

"If you need it—use this—" Rip's face was very sober.

Ali arose from fastening the extra suit in place. "It's ready—"

He came back into the corridor and Dane clanked out in his place, settling himself behind the controls. When they saw him there, the inner hatch closed and he was alone in the bay.

With tantilizing slowness the outer wall of the spacer slid back. His hands, blundering within the metallic claws of the gloves, Dane buckled two safety belts about him. Then the skeleton flitter moved to the left—out into the glare of the early day, a light too bright, even through the shielded viewplates of his helmet.

For some dangerous moment the machine creaked out and down on the landing cranes, the warning counter on its control panel going into a mad whirl of color as it tried to record the radiation. There came a jar as it touched the scorched earth at the foot of the Queen's fins.

Dane pressed the release and watched the lines whip up and the hatch above snap shut. Then he opened the controls. He used too much energy and shot into the air, tearing a wide gap through what was luckily a thin screen of the matted foliage, before he gained complete mastery.

Then he was able to level out and bore westward, the rising sun at his back, the sea of deadly green beneath him, and somewhere far ahead the faint promise of clean, radiation free land holding the help they needed.

Mile after mile of the green jungle swept under the flitter, and the flash of the counter's light continued to record a land unfit for mankind. Even with the equipment used on distant worlds to protect what spacemen had come to recognize was a reasonably tough human frame, no ground force could hope to explore that wilderness in person. And flying above it, as well insulated as he was, Dane knew that he could be dangerously exposed. If the contaminated territory extended more than a thousand miles, his danger was no longer problematical—it was an established fact.

He had only the vague directions from the scrap of map Rip had uncovered. To the west—he had no idea how far away— there stretched a length of coastline, far enough from the radiation blasted area to allow small settlements. For generations the population of Terra, decimated by the atomic wars, and then drained by first system and then Galactic exploration and colonization, had been decreasing. But within the past hundred years it was again on the upswing. Men retiring from space were returning to their native planet to live out their remaining years. The descendants of far-flung colonists, coming home on visits, found the sparsely populated mother world appealed to some basic instinct so that they remained. And now the settlements of mankind were on the march, spreading out from the well established sections which had not been blighted by ancient wars.

It was mid-afternoon when Dane noted that the green carpet beneath the flitter was displaying holes—that small breaks in the vegetation became sizable stretches of rocky waste. He kept one eye on the counter and what, when he left the spacer, had been an almost steady beam of warning light was now a well defined succession of blinks. The land below was cooling off—perhaps he had passed the worst of the journey. But in that passing how much had he and the flitter become contaminated? Ali had devised a method of protection for the empty suit the Medic would wear—had that held? There were an alarming number of dark ifs in the immediate future.

The mutant growths were now only thin patches of stunted and yellowish green. Had man penetrated only this far into the Burn, the knowledge of what lay beyond would be totally false. This effect of dreary waste might well discourage exploration.

Now the blink of the counter was deliberate, with whole seconds of pause between the flashes. Cooling off—? It was getting cold fast! He wished that he had a com-unit. Because of the interference in the Burn he had left it behind—but with one he might be able now to locate some settlement. All that remained was to find the seashore and, with it as a guide, flit south towards the center of modern civilization.

He laid no plans of action—this whole exploit must depend upon improvisation. And, as a Free Trader, spur-of-the-moment action was a necessary way of life. On the frontier Rim of the Galaxy, where the independent spacers traced the star trails, fast thinking and the ability to change plans on an instant were as important as skill in aiming a blaster. And it was very often proven that the tongue—and the brain behind it—were more deadly than a flamer.

The sun was in Dane's face now and he caught sight of patches of uncontaminated earth with honest vegetation—in place of the "hot" jungle now miles behind. That night he camped out on the edge of rough pasturage where the counter no longer flashed its warning and he was able to shed the suit and sleep under the stars with the fresh air of early summer against his cheek and the smell of honest growing things replacing the dry scent of the spacer and the languorous perfumes of Sargol.

He lay on his back, flat against the earth of which he was truly a part, staring up into the dark, inverted bowl of the heavens. It was so hard to connect those distant points of icy light making the well remembered patterns overhead with the suns whose rays had added to the brown stain on his skin. Sargol's sun—the one which gave such limited light to dead Limbo—the sun under which Naxos, his first Galactic port, grew its food. He could not pick them out—was not even sure that any could be sighted from Terra. Strange suns, red, orange, blue, green, white—yet from here all looked alike—points of glitter.

Tomorrow at dawn he must go on. He turned his head away from the sky and grass, green Terran grass, was soft beneath his cheek. Yet unless he was successful tomorrow—or the next day—he might never have the right to feel that grass again.

Resolutely Dane willed that thought out of his mind, tried to fix upon something more lulling which would bring with it the sleep he must have before he went on. And in the end he did sleep, deeply, dreamlessly, as if the touch of Terra's soil was in itself the sedative his tautly strung nerves needed.

It was before sunrise that he awoke, stiff, and chilled. The grayness of pre-dawn gave partial light and somewhere a bird was twittering. There had been birds—or things whose far off ancestors had been birds—in the "hot" forest. Did they also sing to greet the dawn?

Dane went over the flitter with his small counter and was relieved to find that they had done a good job of shielding under Ali's supervision. Once the suit he had worn was stored, he could sit at the controls without danger and in comfort. And it was good to be free of that metal prison.

This time he took to the air with ease, the salt taste of food concentrate on his tongue as he sucked a cube. And his confidence arose with the flitter. This was *the* day, somehow he knew it. He was going to find what he sought.

It was less than two hours after sunrise that he did so. A village which was a cluster of perhaps fifty or so house units strung along the shores of a narrow bay, thrust like an exploring finger into the land. He skimmed across it and brought the flitter down in a rock cliff walled sand pocket with surf booming some yards away, where he would be reasonably sure of safe hiding.

All right, he had found a village. Now what? A Medic— A stranger appearing on the lane which served the town, a stranger in a distinctive uniform of Trade, would only incite conjecture and betrayal. He had to plan now—

Dane unsealed his tunic. He should, by rights, shed his space boots too. But perhaps he could use those to color his story. He thrust the blaster into hiding at his waist. A rip or two in his undertunic, a shallow cut from his bush knife allowed to bleed messily. He could not see himself to judge the general effect, but had to hope it was the right one.

His chance to test his acting powers came sooner than he

had anticipated. Luckily he had climbed out of the hidden cove before he was spotted by the boy who came whistling along the path, a fishing pole over his shoulder, a basket swinging from his hand. Dane assumed an expression which he thought would suggest fatigue, pain, and bewilderment and lurched forward as if, in sighting the oncoming boy, he had also sighted hope.

"Help—!" Perhaps it was excitement which gave his utterance that convincing croak.

Rod and basket fell to the ground as the boy, after one astounded stare, ran forward.

"What's the matter!" His eyes were on those space boots and he added a "sir" which had the ring of hero worship.

"Escape boat—" Dane waved toward the sea's general direction. "Medic—must get to Medic—"

"Yes, sir," the boy's basic Terran sounded good. "Can you walk if I help you?"

Dane managed a weak nod, but contrived that he did not lean too heavily on his avidly helpful guide.

"The Medic's my father, sir. We're right down this slope— third house. And father hasn't left—he's supposed to go on a northern inspection tour today—"

Dane felt a stab of distaste for the role being forced upon him. When he had visualized the Medic he must abduct to serve the Queen in her need, he had not expected to have to kidnap a family man. Only the knowledge that he did have that extra suit, and that he had made the outward trip without dangerous exposure, bolstered up his determination to see the plan through.

When they came out at the end of the single long lane which tied the houses of the village together, Dane was puzzled to see the place so deserted. But, since it was not within his role of dazzed sufferer to ask questions, he did not do so. It was his young guide who volunteered the information he wanted.

"Most everyone is out with the fleet. There's a run of red-backs—"

Dane understood. Within recent times the "red-backs" of the

north had become a desirable luxury item for Terran tables. If a school of them were to be found in the vicinity no wonder this village was now deserted as its fleet went out to garner in the elusive but highly succulent fish.

"In here, sir—" Dane found himself being led to a house on the right. "Are you in Trade—?"

He suppressed a start, shedding his uniform tunic had not done much in the way of disguise. It would be nice, he thought a little bitterly, if he could flash an I-S badge now to completely confuse the issue. But he answered with the partial truth and did not enlarge.

"Yes—"

The boy was flushed with excitement. "I'm trying for Trade Service Medic," he confided. "Passed the Directive exam last month. But I still have to go up for Prelim psycho—"

Dane had a flash of memory. Not too many months before not the Prelim psycho, but the big machine at the Assignment Center had decided his own future arbitrarily, fitting him into the crew of the Solar Queen as the ship where his abilities, knowledge and potentialities could best work to the good of the Service. At the time he had resented, had even been slightly ashamed of being relegated to a Free Trading spacer while Artur Sands and other classmates from the Pool had walked off with Company assignments. Now he knew that he would not trade the smallest and most rusty bolt from the Solar Queen for the newest scout ship in I-S or Combine registry. And this boy from the frontier village might be himself as he was five years earlier. Though he had never known a real home or family, scrapping into the Pool from one of the children's Depots.

"Good luck!" He meant that and the boy's flush deepened.

"Thank you, sir. Around here—Father's treatment room has this other door—"

Dane allowed himself to be helped into the treatment room and sat down in a chair while the boy hurried off to locate the Medic. The Trader's hand went to the butt of his concealed blaster. It was a job he had to do—one he had volunteered for—and there was no backing out. But his mouth had a wry twist as he drew out the blaster and made ready to point it at the inner door. Or—his mind leaped to another idea—could he get the Medic safely out of the village? A story about another man badly injured—perhaps pinned in the wreckage of an escape boat— He could try it. He thrust the blaster back inside his torn undertunic, hoping the bulge would pass unnoticed.

"My son says—"

Dane looked up. The man who came through the inner door was in early middle age, thin, wiry, with a hard, fined-down look about him. He could almost be Tau's elder brother. He crossed the room with a brisk stride and came to stand over Dane, his hand reaching to pull aside the bloody cloth covering the Trader's breast. But Dane fended off that examination.

"My partner," he said. "Back there—pinned in—" he jerked his hand southward. "Needs help—"

The Medic frowned. "Most of the men are out with the fleet. Jorge," he spoke to the boy who had followed him, "go and get Lex and Hartog. Here," he tried to push Dane back into the chair as the Trader got up, "let me look at that cut—"

Dane shook his head. "No time now, sir. My partner's hurt bad. Can you come?"

"Certainly." The Medic reached for the emergency kit on the shelf behind him. "You able to make it?"

"Yes," Dane was exultant. It was going to work! He could toll the Medic away from the village. Once out among the rocks on the shoreline he could pull the blaster and herd the man to the flitter. His luck was going to hold after all!

chapter 15

MEDIC HOVAN REPORTS

Fortunately the path out of the straggling town was a twisted one and in a very short space they were hidden from view. Dane paused as if the pace was too much for an injured man. The Medic put out a steadying hand, only to drop it quickly when he saw the weapon which had appeared in Dane's grip.

"What—?" His mouth snapped shut, his jaw tightened.

"You will march ahead of me," Dane's low voice was steady. "Beyond that rock spur to the left you'll find a place where it is possible to climb down to sea level. Do it!"

"I suppose I shouldn't ask why?"

"Not now. We haven't much time. Get moving!"

The Medic mastered his surprise and without further protest obeyed orders. It was only when they were standing by the flitter and he saw the suits that his eyes widened and he said:

"The Big Burn!"

"Yes, and I'm desperate—"

"You must be—or mad—" The Medic stared at Dane for a

long moment and then shook his head. "What is it? A plague ship?"

Dane bit his lip. The other was too astute. But he did not ask why or how he had been able to guess so shrewdly. Instead he gestured to the suit Ali had lashed beneath the seat in the flitter. "Get into that and be quick about it!"

The Medic rubbed his hand across his jaw. "I think that you might just be desperate enough to use that thing you're brandishing about so melodramatically if I don't," he remarked in a calmly conversational tone.

"I won't kill. But a blaster burn—"

"Can be pretty painful. Yes, I know that, young man. And," suddenly he shrugged, put down his kit and started donning the suit. "I wouldn't put it past you to knock me out and load me aboard if I did say no. All right—"

Suited, he took his place on the seat as Dane directed, and then the Trader followed the additional precaution of lashing the Medic's metal encased arms to his body before he climbed into his own protective covering. Now they could only communicate by sight through the vision plates of their helmets.

Dane triggered the controls and they arose out of the sand and rock hollow just as a party of two men and a boy came hurrying along the top of the cliff—Jorge and the rescuers arriving too late. The flitter spiraled up into the sunlight and Dane wondered how long it would be before this outrage was reported to the nearest Planet Police base. But would any Police cruiser have the hardihood to follow him into the Big Burn? He hoped that the radiation would hold them back.

There was no navigating to be done. The flitter's "memory" should deposit them at the Queen. Dane wondered at what his silent companion was now thinking. The Medic had accepted his kidnaping with such docility that the very ease of their departure began to bother Dane. Was the other expecting a trailer? Had exploration into the Big Burn from the seaside villages been more extensive than reported officially?

He stepped up the power of the flitter to the top notch and saw with some relief that the ground beneath them was now the rocky waste bordering the devastated area. The metal encased figure that shared his seat had not moved, but now the bubble head turned as if the Medic were intent upon the ground flowing beneath them.

The flicker of the counter began and Dane realized that nightfall would find them still air borne. But so far he had not been aware of any pursuit. Again he wished he had the use of a com—only here the radiation would blanket sound with that continuous roar.

Patches of the radiation vegetation showed now and something in the lines of the Medic's tense figure suggested that these were new to him. Afternoon waned as the patches united, spread into the beginning of the jungle as the counter was once more an almost steady light. When evening closed in they were not caught in darkness—for below trees, looping vines, brush, had a pale, evil glow of their own, proclaiming their toxicity with bluish halos. Sometimes pockets of these made a core of light which pulsed, sending warning fingers at the flitter which sped across it.

The hour was close on midnight before Dane sighted the other light, the pink-red of which winked through the ghastly blue-white with a natural and comforting promise, even though it had been meant for an entirely different purpose. The Queen had earthed with her distress lights on and no one had remembered to snap them off. Now they acted as a beacon to draw the flitter to its berth.

Dane brought the stripped flyer down on the fused ground as close to the spot from which he had taken off as he could remember. Now—if those on the spacer would only move fast enough—!

But he need not have worried, his arrival had been anticipated. Above, the rounded side of the spacer bulged as the hatch opened. Lines swung down to fasten their magnetic clamps on the flitter. Then once more they were air borne, swinging up to be warped into the side of the ship. As the outer port of the flitter berth closed Dane reached over and pulled loose the lashing which immobilized his companion. The Medic stood up, a little awkwardly as might any man who wore space armor for the first time.

The inner hatch now opened and Dane waved his captive into the small section which must serve them as a decontamination space. Free at last of the suits, they went through one more improvised hatch to the main corridor of the Queen where Rip and Ali stood waiting, their weary faces lighting as they saw the Medic.

It was the latter who spoke first. "This *is* a plague ship—"

Rip shook his head. "It is *not*, sir. And you're the one who is going to help us prove that."

The man leaned back against the wall, his face expressionless. "You take a rather tough way of trying to get help."

"It was the only way left us. I'll be frank," Rip continued, "we're Patrol Posted."

The Medic's shrewd eyes went from one drawn young face to the next. "You don't look like very desperate criminals," was his comment. "This your full crew?"

"All the rest are your concern. That is—if you will take the job—" Rip's shoulders slumped a little.

"You haven't left me much choice, have you? If there is illness on board, I'm under the Oath—whether you are Patrol Posted or not. What's the trouble?"

They got him down to Tau's laboratory and told him their story. From a slight incredulity his expression changed to an alert interest and he demanded to see, first the patients and then the pests now immured in the deep freeze. Sometime in the middle of this, Dane, overcome by fatigue which was partly relief from tension, sought his cabin and the bunk from which he wearily disposed Sinbad, only to have the purring cat crawl back once more when he had lain down.

And when he awoke, renewed in body and spirit, it was in a new Queen, a ship in which hope and confidence now ruled.

"Hovan's already got it!" Rip told him exultantly. "It's that poison from the little devils' claws right enough! A narcotic—produces some of the affects of deep sleep. In fact—it may have a medical use. He's excited about it—"

"All right," Dane waved aside information which under other circumstances, promising as it did a chance for future trade, would have engrossed him, to ask a question which at the moment seemed far more to the point. "Can he get our men back on their feet?"

A little of Rip's exuberance faded. "Not right away. He's given them all shots. But he thinks they'll have to sleep it off."

"And we have no idea how long that is going to take," Ali contributed.

Time—for the first time in days Dane was struck by that—time! Because of his training a fact he had forgotten in the past weeks of worry now came to mind—their contract with the storm priests. Even if they were able to clear themselves of the plague charge, even if the rest of the crew were speedily restored to health, he was sure that they could not hope to return to Sargol with the promised cargo, the pay for which was already on board the Queen. They would have broken their pledge and there could be no hope of holding to their trading rights on that world—if they were not blacklisted for breaking contract into the bargain. I-S would be able to move in and clean up and probably they could never prove that the Company was behind their misfortunes—though the men of the Queen would always be convinced that that fact was the truth.

"We're going to break contract—" he said aloud and that shook the other two, knocked some of their assurance out of them.

"How about that?" Rip asked Ali.

The acting-engineer nodded. "We have fuel enough to lift from here and maybe set down at Terraport—if we take it careful and cut vectors. We can't lift from there without refueling —and of course the Patrol are going to sit on their hands while we do that—with us Posted! No, put out of your heads any plan for getting back to Sargol within the time limit. Thorson's right—that way we're flamed out!"

Rip slumped in his seat. "So the Eysies can take over after all?"

"As I see it," Dane cut in, "let's just take one thing at a time.

We may have to argue a broken contract out before the Board. But first we have to get off the Posted hook with the Patrol. Have you any idea about how we are going to handle that?"

"Hovan's on our side. In fact if we let him have the bugs to play with he'll back us all the way. He can swear us a clean bill of health before the Medic Control Center."

"How much will that count after we've broken all their regs?" Ali wanted to know. "If we surrender now we're not going to have much chance, no matter what Hovan does or does not swear to. Hovan's a frontier Medic—I won't say that he's not a member in good standing of their association—but he doesn't have top star rating. And with the Eysies and the Patrol on our necks, we'll need more than one Medic's word—"

But Rip looked from the pessimistic Kamil to Dane. Now he asked a question which was more than half statement.

"You've thought of something?"

"I've remembered something," the Cargo-apprentice corrected. "Recall the trick Van pulled on Limbo when the Patrol was trying to ease us out of our rights there after they took over the outlaw hold?"

Ali was impatient. "He threatened to talk to the Video people and broadcast—tell everyone about the ships wrecked by the Forerunner installation and left lying about full of treasure. But what has that to do with us now—? We bargained away our rights on Limbo for the rest of Cam's monopoly on Sargol —not that it's done us much good—"

"The Video," Dane fastened on the important point, "Van threatened publicity which would embarrass the Patrol and he was legally within his rights. We're outside the law now—but publicity might help again. How many earth-side people know of the unwritten law about open war on plague ships? How many who aren't spacemen know that we could be legally pushed into the sun and fried without any chance to prove we're innocent of carrying a new disease? If we could talk loud and clear to the people at large maybe we'd have a chance for a real hearing—"

"Right from the Terraport broadcast station, I suppose?" Ali taunted.

"Why not?"

There was silence in the cabin as the other two chewed upon that and he broke it again:

"We set down here when it had never been done before."

With one brown forefinger Rip traced some pattern known only to himself on the top of the table. Ali stared at the opposite wall as if it were a bank of machinery he must master.

"It just might be whirly enough to work—" Kamil commented softly. "Or maybe we've been spaced too long and the Whisperers have been chattering into our ears. What about it, Rip, could you set us down close enough to the Center Block there?"

"We can try anything once. But we might crash the old girl bringing her in. There's that apron between the Companies' Launching cradles and the Center—. It's clear there and we could give an E signal coming down which would make them stay rid of it. But I won't try it except as a last resort."

Dane noticed that after that discouraging statement Rip made straight for Jellico's record tapes and routed out the one which dealt with Terraport and the landing instructions for that metropolis of the star ships. To land unbidden there would certainly bring them publicity—and to get to the Video broadcast and tell their story would grant them not only world wide, but system wide hearing. News from Terraport was broadcast on every channel every hour of the day and night and not a single viewer could miss their appeal.

But first there was Hovan to be consulted. Would he be willing to back them with his professional knowledge and assurance? Or would their high-handed method of recruiting his services operate against them now? They decided to let Rip ask such questions of the Medic.

"So you're going to set us down in the center of the big jump-off?" was his first comment, as the acting-Captain of the Queen stated their case. "Then you want me to fire my rockets to certify you are harmless. You don't ask for very much, do you, son?"

Rip spread his hands. "I can understand how it looks to you, sir. We grabbed you and brought you here by force. We can't make you testify for us if you decide not to—"

"Can't you?" The Medic cocked an eyebrow at him. "What about this bully boy of yours with his little blaster? He could herd me right up to the telecast, couldn't he? There's a lot of persuasion in one of those nasty little arms. On the other hand, I've a son who's set on taking out on one of these tin pots to go star hunting. If I handed you over to the Patrol he might make some remarks to me in private. You may be Posted, but you don't look like very hardened criminals to me. It seems that you've been handed a bad situation and handled it as best you know. And I'm willing to ride along the rest of the way on your tail blast. Let me see how many pieces you land us in at Terraport and I'll give you my final answer. If luck holds we may have a couple more of your crew present by that time, also—"

They had had no indication that the Queen had been located, that any posse hunting the kidnaped Medic had followed them into the Big Burn. And they could only hope that they would continue to remain unsighted as they upped-ship once more and cruised into a regular traffic lane for earthing at the port. It would be a chancy thing and Ali and Rip spent hours checking the mechanics of that flight, while Dane and the recovering Weeks worked with Hovan in an effort to restore the sleeping crew.

After three visits to the hold and the discovery that the Hoobat had uncovered no more of the pests, Dane caged the angry blue horror and returned it to its usual stand in Jellico's cabin, certain that the ship was clean for Sinbad now confidently prowled the corridors and went into every cabin or storage space Dane opened for him.

And on the morning of the day they had planned for take-off, Hovan at last had a definite response to his treatment. Craig Tau roused, stared dazedly around, and asked a vague question. The fact that he immediately relapsed once more into semi-coma did not discourage the other Medic. Progress had been made and he was now sure that he knew the proper treatment.

They strapped down at zero hour and blasted out of the weird green wilderness they had not dared to explore, lifting into the arch of the sky, depending upon Rip's knowledge to put them safely down again.

Dane once more rode out the take-off at the com-unit, waiting for the blast of radiation born static to fade so that he could catch any broadcast.

"——turned back last night. The high level of radiation makes it almost certain that the outlaws could not have headed into the dangerous central portion. Search is now spreading north. Authorities are inclined to believe that this last outrage may be a clew to the vanished 'Solar Queen,' a plague ship, warned off and Patrol Posted after her crew plundered an E-Stat belonging to the Inter-Solar Corporation. Anyone having any information concerning this ship—or any strange spacer-report at once to the nearest Terrapolice or Patrol station. These men are undoubtedly armed, desperate and dangerous. Do not take chances—report any contact at once to the nearest Terrapolice or Patrol station!"

"That's putting it strongly," Dane commented as he relayed the message. "Good as giving orders for us to be flamed down at sight—"

"Well, if we set down in the right spot," Rip replied, "they can't flame us out without blasting the larger part of Terraport field with us. And I don't think they are going to do that in a hurry."

Dane hoped Shannon was correct in that belief. It would be more chancy than landing at the E-Stat or in the Big Burn—to gauge it just right and put them down on the Terraport apron where they could not be flamed out without destroying too much, where their very position would give them a bargaining point, was going to be a top star job. If Rip could only pull it off!

He could not evaluate the niceties of that flight, he did not understand all Rip was doing. But he did know enough to remain quietly in his place, ask no questions, and await results with a dry mouth and a wildly beating heart. There came a moment when Rip glanced up at him, one hand poised over the control board. The pilot's voice came tersely, thin and queer:

"Pray it out, Dane—here we go!"

Dane heard the shrill of a riding beam, so tearing he had to move his earphones. They must be almost on top of the control tower to get it like that! Rip was planning on a set down where the Queen would block things neatly. He brought his own fingers down on the E-E-Red button to give the last and most powerful warning. That, to be used only when a ship landing was out of control, should clear the ground below. They could only pray it would vacate the port they were still far from seeing.

"Make it a fin-point, Rip," he couldn't repress that one bit of advice. And was glad he had given it when he saw a ghost grin tug for a moment at Rip's full lips.

"Good enough for a check-ride?"

They were riding her flaming jets down as they would on a strange world. Below the port must be wild. Dane counted off the seconds. Two—three—four—five—just a few more and they would be too low to intercept—without endangering innocent coasters and groundhuggers. When the last minute during which they were still vulnerable passed, he gave a sigh of relief. That was one more point on their side. In the earphones was a crackle of frantic questions, a gabble of orders screaming at him. Let them rave, they'd know soon enough what it was all about.

chapter 16

THE BATTLE OF THE VIDEO

Oddly enough, in spite of the tension which must have boiled within him, Rip brought them in with a perfect four fin-point landing—one which, under the circumstances, must win him the respect of master star-star pilots from the Rim. Though Dane doubted whether if they lost, that skill would bring Shannon anything but a long term in the moon mines. The actual jar of their landing contact was mostly absorbed by the webbing of their shock seats and they were on their feet, ready to move almost at once.

The next operation had been planned. Dane gave a glance at the screen. Ringed now about the Queen were the buildings of Terraport. Yes, any attempt to attack the ship would endanger too much of the permanent structure of the field itself. Rip had brought them down—not on the rocket scarred outer landing space—but on the concrete apron between the Assignment Center and the control tower—a smooth strip usually sacred to the parking of officials ground scooters. He speculated as to whether any of the latter had been converted to molten metal by the exhausts of the Queen's descent.

Like the team they had come to be the four active members of the crew went into action. Ali and Weeks were waiting by an inner hatch, Medic Hovan with them. The Engineer-apprentice was bulky in a space suit, and two more of the un-wieldy body coverings waited beside him for Rip and Dane. With fingers which were inclined to act like thumbs they were sealed into what would provide some protection against any blaster or sleep ray. Then with Hovan, conspicuously wearing no such armor, they climbed into one of the ship's crawlers.

Weeks activated the outer hatch and the crane lines plucked the small vehicle out of the Queen, swinging it dizzily down to the blast scored apron.

"Make for the tower—" Rip's voice was thin in the helmet coms.

Dane at the controls of the crawler pulled on as Ali cast off the lines which anchored them to the spacer.

Through the bubble helmet he could see the frenzied activity in the aroused port. An ant hill into which some idle investigator had thrust a stick and given it a turn or two was nothing compared with Terraport after the unorthodox arrival of the Solar Queen.

"Patrol mobile coming in on southeast vector," Ali announced calmly. "Looks like she mounts a portable flamer on her nose—"

"So." Dane changed direction, putting behind him a customs check point, aware as he ground by that stand, of a line of faces at its vision ports. Evasive action—and he'd have to get the top speed from the clumsy crawler.

"Police 'copter over us—" that was Rip reporting.

Well, they couldn't very well avoid *that*. But at the same time Dane was reasonably sure that its attack would not be an overt one—not with the unarmed, unprotected Hovan prominently displayed in their midst.

But there he was too sanguine. A muffled exclamation from Rip made him glance at the Medic beside him. Just in time to see Hovan slump limply forward, about to tumble from the crawler when Shannon caught him from behind. Dane was too familiar with the results of sleep rays to have any doubts as to what had happened.

The P-copter had sprayed them with its most harmless weapon. Only the suits, insulated to the best of their makers' ability against most of the dangers of space, real and anticipated, had kept the three Traders from being overcome as well. Dane suspected that his own responses were a trifle sluggish, that while he had not succumbed to that attack, he had been slowed. But with Rip holding the unconscious Medic in his seat, Thorson continued to head the crawler for the tower and its promise of a system wide hearing for their appeal.

"There's a P-mobile coming in ahead—"

Dane was irritated by that warning from Rip. He had already sighted that black and silver ground car himself. And he was only too keenly conscious of the nasty threat of the snub nosed weapon mounted on its hood, now pointed straight at the oncoming, too deliberate Traders' crawler. Then he saw what he believed would be their only chance— to play once more the same type of trick as Rip had used to earth them safely.

"Get Hovan under cover," he ordered. "I'm going to crash the tower door!"

Hasty movements answered that as the Medic's limp body was thrust under the cover offered by the upper framework of the crawler. Luckily the machine had been built for heavy duty on rugged worlds where roadways were unknown. Dane was sure he could build up the power and speed necessary to take them into the lower floor of the tower—no matter if its door was now barred against them.

Whether his audacity daunted the P-mobile, or whether they held off from an all out attack because of Hovan, Dane could not guess. But he was glad for a few minutes of grace as he raced the protesting engine of the heavy machine to its last and greatest effort. The treads of the crawler bit on the steps leading up to the impressive entrance of the tower. There was a second or two before traction caught and then the driver's heart snapped back into place as the machine tilted its nose up and headed straight for the portal.

They struck the closed doors with a shock which almost hurled them from their seats. But that engraved bronze expanse had not been cast to withstand a head-on blow from a heavy duty off-world vehicle and the leaves tore apart letting them into the wide hall beyond.

"Take Hovan and make for the riser!" For the second time it was Dane who gave the orders. "I have a blocking job to do here." He expected every second to feel the bit of a police blaster somewhere along his shrinking body—could even a space suit protect him now?

At the far end of the corridor were the attendants and visitors, trapped in the building, who had fled in an attempt to find safety at the crashing entrance of the crawler. These flung themselves flat at the steady advance of the two space suited Traders who supported the unconscious Medic between them, using the low-powered anti-grave units on their belts to take most of his weight so each had one hand free to hold a sleep rod. And they did not hesitate to use those weapons— spraying the rightful inhabitants of the tower until all lay unmoving.

Having seen that Ali and Rip appeared to have the situation in hand, Dane turned to his own self-appointed job. He jammed the machine on reverse, maneuvering it with an ease learned by practice on the rough terrain of Limbo, until the gate doors were pushed shut again. Then he swung the machine around so that its bulk would afford an effective bar to keep the door locked for some very precious moments to come. Short of using a flamer full power to cut their way in, no one was going to force an entrance now.

He climbed out of the machine, to discover, when he turned, that the trio from the Queen had disappeared—leaving all possible opposition asleep on the floor. They must have taken a riser to the broadcasting floor. Dane clanked on to join them, carrying in plated fingers their most important weapon to awake public opinion—an improvised cage in which was housed one of the pests from the cargo hold—the proof of their plague-free state which they intended Hovan to present, via the telecast, to the whole system.

Dane reached the shaft of the riser—to find the platform gone. Would either Rip or Ali have presence of mind enough to send it down to him on automatic?

"Rip—return the riser," he spoke urgently into the throat mike of his helmet com.

"Keep your rockets straight," Ali's cool voice was in his earphones, "It's on its way down. Did *you* remember to bring Exhibit A?"

Dane did not answer. For he was very much occupied with another problem. On the bronze doors he had been at such pains to seal shut there had come into being a round circle of dull red which was speedily changing into a coruscating incandescence. They *had* brought a flamer to bear! It would be a very short time now before the Police could come through. That riser—

Afraid of overbalancing in the bulky suit, Dane did not lean forward to stare up into the shaft. But, as his uncertainty reached a fever pitch, the platform descended and he took two steps forward into temporary safety, still clutching the cage. At the first try the thick fingers of his gloved hand slipped from the lever and he hit it again, harder than he intended, so that he found himself being wafted upward with a speed which did not agree with a stomach, even one long accustomed to space flight. And he almost lost his balance when it came to a stop many floors above.

But he had not lost his wits. Before he stepped from the platform he set the dial on a point which would lift the riser to the top of the shaft and hold it there. That might trap the Traders on the broadcasting floor, but it would also insure them time before the forces of the law could reach them.

Dane located the rest of his party in the circular core chamber of the broadcasting section. He recognized a backdrop he had seen thousands of times behind the announcer who introduced the news-casts. In one corner Rip, his suit off, was working over the still relaxed form of the Medic. While Ali, a grim set to his mouth, was standing with a man who wore the insignia of a Com-tech.

"All set?" Rip looked up from his futile ministrations.

Dane put down the cage and began the business of unhooking his own protective covering. "They were burning through the outer doors of the entrance hall when I took off."

"You're not going to get away with this—" that was the Com-tech.

Ali smiled wearily, a stretch of lips in which there was little or no mirth. "Listen, my friend. Since I started to ride rockets I've been told I wasn't going to get away with this or that. Why not be more original? Use what is between those outsize ears of yours. We fought our way in here—we landed at Terraport against orders—we're Patrol Posted. Do you think that one man, one lone man, is going to keep us now from doing what we came to do? And don't look around for any reinforcements. We sprayed both those rooms. You can run the emergency hook-up singlehanded and you're going to. We're Free Traders—Ha," the man had lost some of his assurance as he stared from one drawn young face to another, "I see you begin to realize what that means. Out on the Rim we play rough, and we play for keeps. I know half a hundred ways to set you screaming in three minutes and at least ten of them will not even leave a mark on your skin! Now do we get Service—or don't we?"

"You'll go to the Chamber for this—!" snarled the tech.

"All right. But first we broadcast. Then maybe someday a ship that's run into bad luck'll have a straighter deal than we've had. You get on your post. And we'll have the play back on—remember that. If you don't give us a clear channel we'll know it. How about it, Rip—how's Hovan?"

Rip's face was a mask of worry. "He must have had a full dose. I can't bring him around."

Was this the end to their bold bid? Let each or all of

them go before the screen to plead their case, let them show the caged pest. But without the professional testimony of the Medic, the weight of an expert opinion on their side, they were licked. Well, sometimes luck did not ride a man's fins all the way in.

But some stubborn core within Dane refused to let him believe that they had lost. He went over to the Medic huddled in a chair. To all appearances Hovan was deeply asleep, sunk in the semi-coma the sleep ray produced. And the frustrating thing was that the man himself could have supplied the counter to his condition, given them the instructions how to bring him around. How many hours away was a natural awaking? Long before that their hold on the station would be broken—they would be in the custody of either Police or Patrol.

"He's sunk—" Dane voiced the belief which put an end to their hopes. But Ali did not seem concerned.

Kamil was standing with their captive, an odd expression on his handsome face as if he were striving to recall some dim memory. When he spoke it was to the Com-tech. "You have an HD OS here?"

The other registered surprise. "I think so—"

Ali made an abrupt gesture. "Make sure," he ordered, following the man into another room. Dane looked to Rip for enlightenment.

"What in the Great Nebula is an HD OS?"

"I'm no engineer. It may be some gadget to get us out of here—"

"Such as a pair of wings?" Dane was inclined to be sarcastic. The memory of that incandescent circle on the door some twenty floors below stayed with him. Tempers of Police and Patrol were not going to be improved by fighting their way around or over the obstacles the Traders had arranged to delay them. If they caught up to the outlaws before the latter had their chance for an impartial hearing, the result was not going to be a happy one as far as the Queen's men were concerned.

Ali appeared in the doorway. "Bring Hovan in here."

Together Rip and Dane carried the Medic into a smaller chamber where they found Ali and the tech busy lashing a small, lightweight tube chair to a machine which, to their untutored eyes, had the semblance of a collection of bars. Obeying instructions they seated Hovan in that chair, fastening him in, while the Medic continued to slumber peacefully. Uncomprehendingly Rip and Dane stepped back while, under Ali's watchful eye, the Com-tech made adjustments and finally snapped some hidden switch.

Dane discovered that he dared not watch too closely what followed. Inured as he thought he was to the tricks of Hyperspace, to acceleration and anti-gravity, the oscillation of that swinging seat, the weird swaying of the half-recumbent figure, did things to his sight and to his sense of balance which seemed perilous in the extreme. But when a groan broke through the hum of Ali's mysterious machine, all of them knew that the Engineer-apprentice had found the answer to their problem, that Hovan was waking.

The Medic was bleary-eyed and inclined to stagger when they freed him. And for several minutes he seemed unable to grasp either his surroundings or the train of events which had brought him there.

Long since the Police must have broken into the entrance corridor below. Perhaps they had by now secured a riser which would bring them up. Ali had forced the Com-tech to throw the emergency control which was designed to seal off from the outer world the entire unit in which they now were. But whether that protective device would continue to hold now, none of the three were certain. Time was running out fast.

Supporting the wobbling Hovan, they went back into the panel room and under Ali's supervision the Com-tech took his place at the control board. Dane put the cage with the pest well to the fore on the table of the announcer and waited for Rip to take his place there with the trembling Medic. When Shannon did not move Dane glanced up in surprise— this was no time to hesitate. But he discovered that the attention of both his shipmates was now centered on him. Rip pointed to the seat.

"You're the talk merchant, aren't you?" the acting commander of the Queen asked crisply. "Now's the time to shout the Lingo—"

They couldn't mean—! But it was very evident that they did. Of course, a Cargo-master was supposed to be the spokesman of a ship. But that was in matters of trade. And how could *he* stand there and argue the case for the Queen? He was the newest joined, the greenest member of her crew. Already his mouth was dry and his nerves tense. But Dane didn't know that none of that was revealed by his face or manner. The usual impassiveness which had masked his inner conflicts since his first days at the Pool served him now. And the others never noted the hesitation with which he approached the announcer's place.

Dane had scarcely seated himself, one hand resting on the cage of the pest, before Ali brought down two fingers in the sharp sweep which signaled the Com-tech to duty. Far above them there was a whisper of sound which signified the opening of the play-back. They would be able to check on whether the broadcast was going out or not. Although Dane could see nothing of the system wide audience which he currently faced, he realized that the room and those in it were now visible on every tuned-in video set. Instead of the factual newscast, the listeners were about to be treated to a melodrama which was as wild as their favorite romances. It only needed the break-in of the Patrol to complete the illusion of action-fiction—crime variety.

A second finger moved in his direction and Dane leaned forward. He faced only the folds of a wall wide curtain, but he must keep in mind that in truth there was a sea of faces before him, the faces of those who he and Hovan, working together, must convince if he were to save the Queen and her crew.

He found his voice and it was steady and even, he might

have been outlining some stowage problem for Van Rycke's approval.

"People of Terra—"

Martian, Venusian, Asteroid colonist—inwardly they were still all Terran and on that point he would rest. He was a Terran appealing to his own kind.

"People of Terra, we come before you to ask justice—" from somewhere the words came easily, flowing from his lips to center on a patch of light ahead. And that "justice" rang with a kind of reassurance.

chapter 17

IN CUSTODY

"To those of you who do not travel the star trails our case may seem puzzling—" the words were coming easily. Dane gathered confidence as he spoke, intent on making those others out there know what it meant to be outlawed.

"We are Patrol Posted, outlawed as a plague ship," he confessed frankly. "But this is our true story—"

Swiftly, with a flow of language he had not known he could command, Dane swung into the story of Sargol, of the pest they had carried away from that world. And at the proper moment he thrust a gloved hand into the cage and brought out the wriggling thing which struck vainly with its poisoned talons, holding it above the dark table so that those unseen watchers could witness that dramatic change of color which made it such a menace. Dane continued the story of the Queen's ill-fated voyage—of their forced descent upon the E-Stat.

"Ask the truth of Inter-Solar," he demanded of the audience

beyond those walls. "We were no pirates. They will discover in their records the vouchers we left." Then Dane described the weird hunt when, led by the Hoobat, they had finally found and isolated the menace, and their landing in the heart of the Big Burn. He followed that with his own quest for medical aid and the kidnaping of Hovan. At that point he turned to the Medic.

"This is Medic Hovan. He has consented to appear in our behalf and to testify to the truth—that the Solar Queen has not been stricken by some unknown plague, but infested with a living organism we now have under control—" For a suspenseful second or two he wondered if Hovan was going to make it. The man looked shaken and sick, as if the drastic awaking they had subjected him to had left him too dazed to pull himself together.

But out of some hidden reservoir of strength the Medic summoned the energy he needed. And his testimony was all they had hoped it would be. Though now and then he strayed into technical terms. But, Dane thought, their use only enhanced the authority of his description of what he had discovered on board the spacer and what he had done to counteract the power of the poison. When he had done Dane added a few last words.

"We have broken the law," he admitted forthrightly, "but we were fighting in self-defense. All we ask now is the privilege of an impartial investigation, a chance to defend ourselves— such as any of you take for granted on Terra—before the courts of this planet—" But he was not to finish without interruption.

From the play-back over their heads another voice blared, breaking across his last words:

"Surrender! This is the Patrol. Surrender or take the consequences!" And that faint sighing which signaled their open contact with the outer world was cut off. The Com-tech turned away from the control board, a sneering half smile on his face.

"They've reached the circuit and cut you off. You're done!"

Dane stared into the cage where the now almost invisible

thing sat humped together. He had done his best—they had all done their best. He felt nothing but a vast fatigue, an overwhelming weariness, not so much of body, but of nerve and spirit too.

Rip broke the silence with a question aimed at the tech. "Can you signal below?"

"Going to give up?" The fellow brightened. "Yes, there's an inter-com I can cut in."

Rip stood up. He unbuckled the belt about his waist and laid it on the table—disarming himself. Without words Ali and Dane followed his example. They had played their hand—to prolong the struggle would mean nothing. The acting Captain of the Queen gave a last order:

"Tell them we are coming down—unarmed—to surrender." He paused in front of Hovan. "You'd better stay here. If there's any trouble—no reason for you to be caught in the middle."

Hovan nodded as the three left the room. Dane, remembering the trick he had pulled with the riser, made a comment:

"We may be marooned here—"

Ali shrugged. "Then we can just wait and let them collect us." He yawned, his dark eyes set in smudges. "I don't care if they'll just let us sleep the clock around afterwards. D'you really think," he addressed Rip, "that we've done ourselves any good?"

Rip neither denied nor confirmed. "We took our only chance. Now it's up to them—" He pointed to the wall and the teeming world which lay beyond it.

Ali grinned wryly. "I note you left the what-you-call-it with Hovan."

"He wanted one to experiment with," Dane replied. "I thought he'd earned it."

"And now here comes what we've earned—" Rip cut in as the hum of the riser came to their ears.

"Should we take to cover?" Ali's mobile eyebrows underlined his demand. "The forces of law and order may erupt with blasters blazing."

But Rip did not move. He faced the riser door squarely

and, drawn by something in that stance of his, the other two stepped in on either side so that they fronted the dubious future as a united group. Whatever came now, the Queen's men would meet it together.

In a way Ali was right. The four men who emerged all had their blasters or riot stun-rifles at ready, and the sights of those weapons were trained at the middles of the Free Traders. As Dane's empty hands, palm out, went up on a line with his shoulders, he estimated the opposition. Two were in the silver and black of the Patrol, two wore the forest green of the Terrapolice. But they all looked like men with whom it was better not to play games.

And it was clear they were prepared to take no chances with the outlaws. In spite of the passiveness of the Queen's men, their hands were locked behind them with force bars about their wrists. When a quick search revealed that the three were unarmed, they were herded onto the riser by two of their captors, while the other pair remained behind, presumably to uncover any damage they had done to the Tower installations.

The police did not speak except for a few terse words among themselves and a barked order to march, delivered to the prisoners. Very shortly they were in the entrance hall facing the wreckage of the crawler and doors through which a ragged gap had been burned. Ali viewed the scene with his usual detachment.

"Nice job," he commended Dane's enterprise. "They'll have a moving—"

"Get going!" A heavy hand between his shoulder blades urged him on.

The Engineer-apprentice whirled, his eyes blazing. "Keep your hands to yourself! We aren't mine fodder yet. I think that the little matter of a trial comes first—"

"You're Posted," the Patrolman was openly contemptuous.

Dane was chilled. For the first time that aspect of their predicament really registered. Posted outlaws might, within reason, be shot on sight without further recourse to the law. If that label stuck on the crew of the Queen, they had practically no chance at all. And when he saw that Ali was no longer inclined to retort, he knew that fact had dawned upon Kamil also. It would all depend upon how big an impression their broadcast had made. If public opinion veered to their side—then they could defend themselves legally. Otherwise the moon mines might be the best sentence they dare hope for.

They were pushed out into the brilliant sunlight. There stood the Queen, her meteor scarred sides reflecting the light of her native sun. And ringed around her at a safe distance was what seemed to be a small mechanized army corps. The authorities were making very sure that no more rebels would burst from her interior.

Dane thought that they would be loaded into a mobile or 'copter and taken away. But instead they were marched down, through the ranks of portable flamers, scramblers, and other equipment, to an open space where anyone on duty at the visa-screen within the control cabin of the spacer could see them. An officer of the Patrol, the sun making an eye-blinding flash of his lightning sword breast badge, stood behind a loud speaker. When he perceived that the three prisoners were present, he picked up a hand mike and spoke into it—his voice so being relayed over the field as clearly as it must be reaching Weeks inside the sealed frighter.

"You have five minutes to open hatch. Your men have been taken. Five minutes to open hatch and surrender."

Ali chuckled. "And how does he think he's going to enforce that?" he inquired of the air and incidentally of the guards now forming a square about the three. "He'll need more than a flamer to unlatch the old girl if she doesn't care for his offer."

Privately Dane agreed with that. He hoped that Weeks would decide to hold out—at least until they had a better idea of what the future would be. No tool or weapon he saw in the assembly about them was forceful enough to penetrate the shell of the Queen. And there were sufficient supplies on board to keep Weeks and his charges going for at least a week. Since Tau had shown signs of coming out of his coma, it might even be that the crew of the ship would arouse to their own defense in that time. It all depended upon Weeks' present decision.

No hatch yawned in the ship's sleek sides. She might have been an inert derelict for all response to that demand. Dane's confidence began to rise. Weeks had picked up the challenge, he would continue to baffle police and Patrol.

Just how long that stalemate would have lasted they were not to know for another player came on the board. Through the lines of besiegers Hovan, escorted by the Patrolmen, made his way up to the officer at the mike station. There was something in his air which suggested that he was about to give battle. And the conversation at the mike was relayed across the field, a fact of which they were not at once aware.

"There are sick men in there—" Hovan's voice boomed out. "I demand the right to return to duty—"

"If and when they surrender they shall all be accorded necessary aid," that was the officer. But he made no impression on the Medic from the frontier. Dane, by chance, had chosen better support than he had guessed.

"Pro Bono Publico—" Hovan invoked the battle cry of his own Service. "For the Public Good—"

"A plague ship—" the officer was beginning. Hovan waved that aside impatiently.

"Nonsense!" His voice scaled up across the field. "There is no plague aboard. I am willing to certify that before the Council. And if you refuse these men medical attention— which they need—I shall cite the case all the way to my Board!"

Dane drew a deep breath. That *was* taking off on their orbit! Not being one of the Queen's crew, in fact having good reason to be angry over his treatment at their hands, Hovan's present attitude would or should carry weight.

The Patrol officer who was not yet ready to concede all points had an answer: "If you are able to get on board—go."

Hovan snatched the mike from the astonished officer.

"Weeks!" His voice was imperative. "I'm coming aboard—alone!"

All eyes were on the ship and for a short period it would seem that Weeks did not trust the Medic. Then, high in her needle nose, one of the escape ports, not intended for use except in dire emergncy opened and allowed a plastic link ladder to fall link by link.

Out of the corner of his eye Dane caught a flash of movement to his left. Manacled as he was he threw himself on the policeman who was aiming a stun rifle into the port. His shoulder struck the fellow waist high and his weight carried them both with a bruising crash to the concrete pavement as Rip shouted and hands clutched roughly at the now helpless Cargo-apprentice.

He was pulled to his feet, tasting the flat sweetness of blood where a flailing blow from the surprised and frightened policeman had cut his lip against his teeth. He spat red and glowered at the ring of angry men.

"Why don't you kick him?" Ali inquired, a vast and blistering contempt sawtoothing his voice. "He's got his hands cuffed so he's fair game—"

"What's going on here?" An officer broke through the ring. The policeman, on his feet once more, snatched up the rifle Dane's attack had knocked out of his hold.

"Your boy here," Ali was ready with an answer, "tried to find a target inside the hatch. Is this the usual way you conduct a truce, sir?"

He was answered by a glare and the rifleman was abruptly ordered to the rear. Dane, his head clearing, looked at the Queen. Hovan was climbing the ladder—he was within arm's length of that half open hatch. The very fact that the Medic had managed to make his point stick was, in a faint way, encouraging. But the three were not allowed to enjoy that small victory for long. They were marched from the field, loaded into a mobile and taken to the city several miles away. It was the Patrol who held them in custody—not the Terrapolice. Dane was not sure whether that was to be reckoned favorable or not. As a Free Trader he had a grudging respect for the organization he had seen in action on Limbo.

Sometime later they found themselves, freed of the force bars, alone in a room which, bare walled as it was, did have a bench on which all three sank thankfully. Dane caught the warning gesture from Ali—they were under unseen observation and they must have a listening audience too—located somewhere in the maze of offices.

"They can't make up their minds," the Engineer-apprentice settled his shoulders against the wall. "Either we're desperate criminals, or we're heroes. They're going to let time decide."

"If we're heroes," Dane asked a little querulously, "what are we doing locked up here? I'd like a few earth-side comforts—beginning with a full meal—"

"No thumb printing, no psycho testing," Rip mused. "Yes, they haven't put us through the system yet."

"And we decidedly aren't the forgotten men. Wipe your face, child," Ali said to Dane, "you're still dribbling."

The Cargo-apprentice smeared his hand across his chin and brought it away red and sticky. Luckily his teeth remained intact.

"We need Hovan to read them more law," observed Kamil. "You should have medical attention."

Dane dabbed at his mouth. He didn't need all that solicitude, but he guessed that Ali was talking for the benefit of those who now kept them under surveillance.

"Speaking of Hovan—I wonder what became of that pest he was supposed to have under control. He didn't bring the cage with him when he came out of the Tower, did he?" asked Rip.

"If it gets loose in that building," Dane decided to give the powers who held them in custody something to think about, "they'll have trouble. Practically invisible and poisonous. And maybe it can reproduce its kind, too. We don't know anything about it—"

Ali laughed. "Such fun and games! Imagine a hundred of the dear creatures flitting in and out of the broadcasting section.

And Captain Jellico has the only Hoobat on Terra! He can name his own terms for rounding up the plague. The whole place will be filled with sleepers before they're through—"

Would that scrap of information send some Patrolmen hurtling off to the Tower in search of the caged creature? The thought of such an expedition was, in a small way, comforting to the captives.

An hour or so later they were fed, noiselessly and without visible attendants, when three trays slid through a slit in the wall at floor level. Rip's nose wrinkled.

"Now I get the vector! We're plague-ridden—keep aloof and watch to see if we break out in purple spots!"

Ali was lifting thermo lids from the containers and now he suddenly arose and bowed in the direction of the blank wall. "Many, many thanks," he intoned. "Nothing but the best—a sub-commander's rations at least! We shall deliver top star rating to this thoughtfulness when we are questioned by the powers that shine."

It *was* good food. Dane ate cautiously because of his torn lip, but the whole adventure took on a more rose-colored hue. The lapse of time before they were put through the usual procedure followed with criminals, this excellent dinner—it was all promising. The Patrol could not yet be sure how they were to be handled.

"They've fed us," Ali observed as he clanged the last dish back on a tray. "Now you'd think they'd bed us. I could do with several days—and nights—of bunk time right about now."

But that hint was not taken up and they continued to sit on the bench as time limped by. According to Dane's watch it must be night now, though the steady light in the windowless room did not vary. What had Hovan discovered in the Queen? Had he been able to rouse any of the crew? And was the spacer still inviolate, or had the Terrapolice and the Patrol managed to take her over?

He was so very tired, his eyes felt as if hot sand had been poured beneath the lids, his body ached. And at last he nodded into naps from which he awoke with jerks of the neck. Rip was frankly asleep, his shoulders and head resting against the wall, while Ali lounged with closed eyes. Though the Cargo-apprentice was sure that Kamil was more alert than his comrades, as if he waited for something he thought was soon to occur.

Dane dreamed. Once more he trod the reef rising out of Sargol's shallow sea. But he held no weapon and beneath the surface of the water a gorp lurked. When he reached the break in the water-washed rock just ahead, the spidery horror would strike and against its attack he was defenseless. Yet he must march on for he had no control over his own actions!

"Wake up!" Ali's hand was on his shoulder, shaking him back and forth with something close to gentleness. "Must you give an imitation of a space-whirly moonbat?"

"The gorp—" Dane came back to the present and flushed. He dreaded admitting to a nightmare—especially to Ali whose poise he had always found disconcerting.

"No gorps here. Nothing but—"

Kamil's words were lost in the scrape of metal against metal as a panel slid back in the wall. But no guard wearing the black and silver of the Patrol stepped through to summon them to trial. Van Rycke stood in the opening, half smiling at them with his customary sleepy benevolence.

"Well, well, and here're our missing ones," his purring voice was the most beautiful sound Dane thought he had ever heard.

chapter 18

BARGAIN CONCLUDED

"—and so we landed here, sir," Rip concluded his report in the matter-of-fact tone he might have used in describing a perfectly ordinary voyage, say between Terraport and Luna City, a run of no incident and dull cargo carrying.

The crew of the Solar Queen, save for Tau, were assembled in a room somewhere in the vastness of Patrol Headquarters. Since the room seemed a comfortable conference chamber, Dane thought that their status must now be on a higher level than that of Patrol Posted outlaws. But he was also sure that if they attempted to walk out of the building that effort would not be successful.

Van Rycke sat stolidly in his chosen seat, fingers of both hands laced across his substantial middle. He had sat as impassively as the Captain while Rip had outlined their adventures since they had all been stricken. Though the other listeners had betrayed interest in the story, the senior officers made no comments. Now Jellico turned to his Cargo-master.

"How about it, Van?"

"What's done is done—"

Dane's elation vanished as if ripped away by a Sargolian storm wind. The Cargo-master didn't approve. So there must have been another way to achieve their ends—one the younger members of the crew had been too inexperienced or too dense to see—

"If we blasted off today we might just make cargo contract."

Dane started. That was it! The point they had lost sight of during their struggles to get aid. There was no possible chance of upping the ship today—probably not for days to come—or ever, if the case went against them. So they had broken contract —and the Board would be down on them for that. Dane shivered inside. He could try to fight back against the Patrol— there had always been a slight feeling of rivalry between the Free Traders and the space police. But you couldn't buck the Board—and keep your license and so have a means of staying in space. A broken contract could cut one off from the stars forever. Captain Jellico looked very bleak at that reminder.

"The Eysies will be all ready to step in. I'd like to know why they were so sure we had the plague on board—"

Van Rycke snorted. "I can supply you five answers to that —for one they may have known the affinity of those creatures for the wood, and it would be easy to predict as a result of our taking a load on board—or again they may have deliberately planted the things on us through the Salariki— But we can't ever prove it. It remains that they are going to get for themselves the Sargolian contract unless—" He stopped short, staring straight ahead of him at the wall between Rip and Dane. And his assistant knew that Van was exploring a fresh idea. Van's ideas were never to be despised and Jellico did not now disturb the Cargo-master with questions.

It was Rip who spoke next and directly to the Captain. "Do you know what they plan to do about us, sir?"

Captain Jellico grunted and there was a sardonic twist to his mouth as he replied, "It's my opinion that they're now busy adding up the list of crimes you four have committed—maybe they had to turn the big HG computer loose on the problem. The tally isn't in yet. We gave them our automat flight record and that ought to give them more food for thought."

Dane speculated as to what the experts *would* make of the mechanical record of the Queen's past few weeks—the section dealing with their landing in the Big Burn ought to be a little surprising. Van Rycke got to his feet and marched to the door of the conference room. It was opened from without so quickly Dane was sure that they had been under constant surveillance.

"Trade business," snapped the Cargo-master, "contract deal. Take me to a sealed com booth!"

Contracts might not be as sacred to the protective Service as they were to Trade, but Trade had its powers and since Van Rycke, an innocent bystander of the the Queen's troubles, could not legally be charged with any crime, he was escorted out of the room. But the door panel was sealed behind him, shutting in the rest with the unspoken warning that they were not free agents. Jellico leaned back in his chair and stretched. Long years of close partnership had taught him that his Cargo-master was to be trusted with not only the actual trading and cargo tending, but could also think them out of some of the tangles which could not be solved by his own direct action methods. Direct action had been applied to their present problem—now the rest was up to Van, and he was willing to delegate all responsibility.

But they were not left long to themselves. The door opened once more to admit star rank Patrolmen. None of the Free Traders arose. As members of another Service they considered themselves equals. And it was their private boast that the interests of Galactic civilization, as represented by the black and silver, often followed, not preceded the brown tunics into new quarters of the universe.

However, Rip, Ali, Dane, and Weeks answered as fully as they could the flood of questions which engulfed them. They explained in detail their visit to the E-Stat, the landing in the Big Burn, the kidnaping of Hovan. Dane's stubborn feeling of being in the right grew in opposition to the questioning. Under the same set of circumstances how would that Commander—that Wing Officer—that Senior Scout—now all seated there—have acted? And every time they inferred that his part in the affair had been illegal he stiffened.

Sure, there had to be law and order out on the Rim—and doubly sure it had to cover and protect life on the softer planets of the inner systems. He wasn't denying that on Limbo, he, for one, had been very glad to see the Patrol blast their way into the headquarters of the pirates holed up on that half-dead world. And he was never contemptuous of the men in the field. But like all Free Traders he was influenced by a belief that too often the laws as enforced by the Patrol favored the wealth and might of the Companies, that law could be twisted and the Patrol sent to push through actions which, though legal, were inherently unfair to those who had not the funds to fight it out in the far off Council courts. Just as now he was certain that the Eysies were bringing all the influence they had to bear here against the Queen's men. And Inter-Solar had a lot of influence.

At the end of their ordeal their statements were read back to them from the recording tape and they thumb signed them. Were these statements or confessions, Dane mused. Perhaps in their honest reports they had just signed their way into the moon mines. Only there was no move to lead them out and book them. And when Weeks pressed his thumb at the bottom of the tape, Captain Jellico took a hand. He looked at his watch.

"It is now ten hours," he observed. "My men need rest, and we all want food. Are you through with us?"

The Commander was spokesman for the other group. "You are to remain in quarantine, Captain. Your ship has not yet been passed as port-free. But you will be assigned quarters—"

Once again they were marched through blank halls to the other section of the sprawling Patrol Headquarters. No windows looked upon the outer world, but there were bunks and a small mess alcove. Ali, Dane, and Rip turned in, more interested in sleep than food. And the last thing the Cargo-apprentice remembered was seeing Jellico talking earnestly with Steen Wilcox as they both sipped steaming mugs of real Terran coffee.

But with twelve hours of sleep behind them the three were less contented in confinement. No one had come near them and Van Rycke had not returned. Which fact the crew clung to as a ray of hope. Somewhere the Cargo-master must be fighting their battle. And all Van's vast store of Trade knowledge, all his knack of cutting corners and driving a shrewd bargain, enlisted on their behalf, must win them some concessions.

Medic Tau came in, bringing Hovan with him. Both looked tired but triumphant. And their report was a shot in the arm for the now uneasy Traders.

"We've rammed it down their throats," Tau announced. "They're willing to admit that it was those poison bugs and not a plague. Incidentally," he grinned at Jellico and then looked around expectantly, "where's Van? This comes in his department. We're going to cash in on those the kids dumped in the deep freeze. Terra-Lab is bidding on them. I said to see Van—he can arrange the best deal for us. Where is he?"

"Gone to see about our contract," Jellico reported. "What's the news about our status now?"

"Well, they've got to wipe out the plague ship listing. Also—we're big news. There're about twenty video men rocketing around out in the offices trying to get in and have us do some spot broadcasts. Seems that the children here," he jerked his thumb at the three apprentices, "started something. An inter solar invasion couldn't be bigger news! Human interest by the tankful. I've been on Video twice and they're trying to sign up Hovan almost steady—"

The Medic from the frontier nodded. "Wanted me to appear on a three week schedule," he chuckled. "I was asked to come in on 'Our Heroes of the Starlines' and two Quizz programs. As for you, you young criminal," he swung to Dane, "you're going to be fair game for about three networks. It seems you transmit well," he uttered the last as if it were an accusation and Dane squirmed. "Anyway you did something with your crazy stunt. And, Captain, three men want to buy your Hoobat. I gather they are planning a showing of how it captures those pests. So be prepared—"

Dane tried to visualize a scene in which he shared top billing with Queex and shuddered. All he wanted now was to get free of Terra for a nice, quiet, uncomplicated world where problems could be settled with a sleep rod or a blaster and the Video screen was unknown.

Having heard of what awaited them—without the men of the Queen—were more content to be incarcerated in the quarantine section. But as time wore on and the Cargo-master did not return, their anxieties awoke. They were fairly sure by now that any penalty the Patrol or the Terrapolice would impose would not be too drastic. But a broken contract was another and more serious affair—a matter which might ground them more effectively than any rule of the law enforcement bodies. And Jellico took to pacing the room, while Tang and Wilcox who had started a game of four dimensional chess made countless errors of move, and Stotz stared moodily at the wall, apparently too sunk in his own gloomy thoughts to rise from the mess table in the alcove.

Though time had ceased to have much meaning for them except as an irritating reminder of the now sure failure of their Sargolian venture, they marked the hours into a second full day of detention before Van Rycke finally put in appearance. The Cargo-master was plainly tired, but he showed no signs of discomposure. In fact as he came in he was humming what he fondly imagined was a popular tune.

Jellico asked no questions, he merely regarded his trusted officer with a quizzically raised eyebrow. But the others drew around. It was so apparent that Van Rycke was pleased with himself. Which could only mean that in some fantastic way he had managed to bring their venture down in a full fin landing, that somehow he had argued the Queen out of danger into a position where he could control the situation.

He halted just within the doorway and eyed Dane, Ali, and Rip with mock severity. "You're baaaad boys," he told them with a shake of the head and a drawl of the adjective. "You've been demoted ten files each on the list."

Which must put him on the bottom rung once more, Dane calculated swiftly. Or even below—though he didn't see how he could fall beneath the rank he held at assignment. However he found the news heartening instead of discouraging. Compared to a bleak sentence at the moon mines such demotion was absolutely nothing and he knew that Van Rycke was breaking the worst news first.

"You also forfeit all pay for this voyage," the Cargo-master was continuing. But Jellico broke in.

"Board fine?"

At the Cargo-master's nod, Jellico added. "Ship pays that."

"So I told them," Van Rycke agreed. "The Queen's warned off Terra for ten solar years—"

They could take that, too. Other Free Traders got back to their home ports perhaps once in a quarter century. It was so much less than they had expected that that sentence was greeted with a concentrated sigh of relief.

"No earth-side leave—"

All right—no leave. They were not, after their late experiences so entranced with Terraport that they wanted to linger in its environs any longer than they had to.

"We lose the Sargol contract—"

That did hurt. But they had resigned themselves to it since the hour when they had realized that they could not make it back to the perfumed planet.

"To Inter-Solar?" Wilcox asked the important question.

Van Rycke was smiling broadly, as if the loss he had just announced was in some way a gain. "No—to Combine!"

"Combine?" the Captain echoed and his puzzlement was duplicated around the circle. How did Inter-Solar's principal rival come into it?

"We've made a deal with Combine," Van Rycke informed them. "I wasn't going to let I-S cash in on our loss. So I went to Vickers at Combine and told him the situation. He understands that we were in solid with the Salariki and that the Eysies are not. And a chance to point a blaster at I-S's tail is just what he has been waiting for. The shipment will go out to the storm priests tomorrow on a light cruiser—it'll make it on time."

Yes, a light cruiser, one of the fast ships maintained by the big Companies, could make the transition to Sargol with a slight margin to spare. Stotz nodded his approval at this practical solution.

"I'm going with it—" That did jerk them all up short. For Van Rycke to leave the Queen—*that* was as unthinkable as if Captain Jellico had suddenly announced that he was about to retire and become a kelp farmer. "Just for the one trip," the Cargo-master hastened to assure them. "I smooth their vector with the storm priests and hand over so the Eysies will be frozen out—"

Captain Jellico interrupted at that point. "D'you mean that Combine is *buying* us out—not just taking over? What kind of a deal—"

But Van Rycke, his smile a brilliant stretch across his plump face, was nodding in agreement. "They're taking over our contract and our place with the Salariki."

"In return for what?" Steen Wilcox asked for them all.

"For twenty-five thousand credits and a mail run between Xecho and Trewsworld—frontier planets. They're far enough from Terra to get around the exile ruling. The Patrol will escort us out and see that we get down to work like good little space men. We'll have two years of a nice, quiet run on regular pay. Then, when all the powers that shine have forgotten about us, we can cut in on the trade routes again."

"And the pay?" "First or second class mail?" "When do we start?"

"Standard pay on the completion of each run—Board rates," he made replies in order. "First, second and third class mail— anything that bears the government seal and out in those quarters it is apt to be *anything*! And you start as soon as you

can get to Xecho and relieve the Combine scout which has
been holding down the run."

"While you go to Sargol—" commented Jellico.

"While I make one voyage to Sargol. You can spare me,"
he dropped one of his big hands on Dane's shoulder and gave
the flesh beneath it a quick squeeze. "Seeing as how our juniors
helped pull us out of this last mix-up we can trust them about
an inch farther than we did before. Anyway—Cargo-master
on a mail run is more or less a thumb-twiddling job at the best.
And you can trust Thorson on stowage—that's one thing he
does know." Which dubious ending left Dane wondering as to
whether he had been complimented or warned. "I'll be on
board again before you know it—the Combine will ship me
out to Trewsworld on your second trip across and I'll join
ship there. For once we won't have to worry for awhile. Nothing can happen on a mail run." He shook his head at the
three youngest members of the crew. "You're in for a very dull
time—and it will serve you right. Give you a chance to learn
your jobs so that when you come up for reassignment you
can pick up some of those files you were just demoted. Now,"
he started briskly for the door. "I'll tranship to the Combine
cruiser. I take it that you *don't* want to meet the Video people?"

At their hasty agreement to that, he laughed. "Well, the
Patrol doesn't want the Video spouting about 'high-handed
official news suppression' so about an hour or so from now
you'll be let out the back way. They put the Queen in a cradle
and a field scooter will take you to her. You'll find her serviced
for a take-off to Luna City. You can refit there for deep space.
Frankly the sooner you get off-world the happier all ranks are
going to be—both here and on the Board. It will be better
for us to walk softly for a while and let them forget that the
Solar Queen and her crazy crew exists. Separately and together
you've managed to break—or at least bend—half the laws in
the books and they'd like to have us out of their minds."

Captain Jellico stood up. "They aren't any more anxious to
see us go than we are to get out of here. You've pulled it off

for us again, Van, and we're lucky to get out of it this easy—"

Van Rycke rolled his eyes ceilingward. "You'll never know how lucky! Be glad Combine hates the space I-S blasts through. We were able to use that to our advantage. Get the big fellows at each others' throats and they'll stop annoying us—simple proposition but it works. Anyway we're set in blessed and peaceful obscurity now. Thank the Spirit of Free Space there's practically no trouble one can get into on a safe and sane mail route!"

But Cargo-master Van Rycke, in spite of knowing the Solar Queen and the temper of her crew, was exceedingly overoptimistic when he made that emphatic statement.